Muriel Spark

Bang-bang You're Dead

and other stories

GRANADA

London Toronto Sydney New York

Published by Granada Publishing Limited in 1982

ISBN 0 586 05578 9

This collection a Granada Paperback Original
Copyright © Copyright Administration Limited 1960, 1961,
1963, 1966, 1967, 1975, 1981

Granada Publishing Limited
Frogmore, St Albans, Herts AL2 2NF
and
36 Golden Square, London W1R 4AH
866 United Nations Plaza, New York, NY 10017, USA
117 York Street, Sydney, NSW 2000, Australia
100 Skyway Avenue, Rexdale, Ontario, M9W 3A6, Canada
61 Beach Road, Auckland, New Zealand

Printed and bound in Great Britain by
Cox and Wyman Ltd, Reading
Set in Baskerville

Granada ®
Granada Publishing ®

Muriel Spark was born and educated in Edinburgh, and spent some years in Central Africa. She returned to Britain during the war and worked in the Political Intelligence Department of the Foreign Office. She subsequently edited two poetry magazines, and her published works include critical biographies of nineteenth-century figures, and editions of nineteenth-century letters. Her *Collected Poems I* and *Collected Stories I* were published in 1967. Since she won an *Observer* short-story competition in 1951 her creative writings have achieved international recognition (they are published in more than twenty different languages). Among many other awards she has received the Italia Prize and the James Tait Black Memorial Prize. She was awarded the O.B.E. in 1967.

Mrs Spark became a Roman Catholic in 1954. She has one son.

Her first novel, *The Comforters*, was published in 1957 and this was followed by *Robinson* (1958), *The Go-Away Bird and Other Stories* (1958), *Memento Mori* (1959), *The Ballad of Peckham Rye* (1960), *The Bachelors* (1960), *Voices at Play* (1961), *The Prime of Miss Jean Brodie* (1961), adaptations of which have enjoyed long and successful runs on the stage and the screen. *The Girls of Slender Means* (1963), *The Mandelbaum Gate* (1965), *The Public Image* (1968), *The Driver's Seat* (1970), *Not to Disturb* (1971), *The Hothouse by the East River* (1973), *The Abbess of Crewe* (1974), *The Takeover* (1976), *Territorial Rights* (1979) and *Loitering with Intent* (1981).

Her play *Doctors of Philosophy* was first produced in London in 1962 and published in 1963.

By the same author

Novels
The Comforters
Robinson
Memento Mori
The Bachelors
The Ballad of Peckham Rye
The Prime of Miss Jean Brodie
The Girls of Slender Means
The Mandelbaum Gate
The Public Image
The Driver's Seat
Not to Disturb
The Hothouse by the East River
The Abbess of Crewe
The Takeover
Territorial Rights
Loitering with Intent

Play
Doctors of Philosophy

Criticism and Biography
The Brontë Letters
John Masefield
Child of Light

Poetry
Collected Poems I

Stories
Collected Stories I
The Go-Away Bird

For Children
The Very Fine Clock

Contents

Acknowledgements

The following stories appeared in 'Winter's Tales': *The Gentile Jewesses* (No 9, 1963), *The House of the Famous Poet* (No 12, 1966), *The First Year of My Life* (No 21, 1975).

A Member of the Family, appeared in Vogue (UK) and Mademoiselle.

The following stories appeared in The New Yorker: *The Ormolu Clock*, *The House of the Famous Poet*, *Alice Long's Dachshunds*, *The Gentile Jewesses*, *The First Year of My Life*.

All the stories, with the exception of *The Gentile Jewesses* and *The First Year of My Life*, have appeared in COLLECTED STORIES I, first published by Macmillan in 1967.

Bang-bang You're Dead

At that time many of the men looked like Rupert Brooke, whose portrait still hung in everyone's imagination. It was that clear-cut, 'typically English' face which is seldom seen on the actual soil of England but proliferates in the African Colonies.

'I must say,' said Sybil's hostess, 'the men look charming.'

These men were all charming, Sybil had decided at the time, until you got to know them. She sat in the dark-room watching the eighteen-year-old microfilm unrolling on the screen as if the particular memory had solidified under the effect of some intense heat coming out of the projector. She told herself, I was young, I demanded nothing short of perfection. But then, she thought, that is not quite the case. But it comes to the same thing; to me, the men were not charming for long.

The first reel came to an end. Someone switched on the light. Her host picked the next film out of its tropical packing.

'It must be an interesting experience,' said her hostess, 'seeing yourself after all those years.'

'Hasn't Sybil seen these films before?' said a latecomer.

'No, never – have you, Sybil?'

'No, never.'

'If they had been my films,' said her hostess, 'my curiosity could not have waited eighteen years.'

The Kodachrome reels had lain in their boxes in the dark of Sybil's cabin trunk. Why bother, when one's memory was clear?

'Sybil didn't know anyone who had a projector,' said her hostess, 'until we got ours.'

'It was delightful,' said the latecomer, an elderly lady, 'what I saw of it. Are the others as good?'

Sybil thought for a moment. 'The photography is probably good,' she said. 'There was a cook behind the camera.'

'A cook! How priceless; whatever do you mean?' said her hostess.

'The cook-boy,' said Sybil, 'was trained up to use the camera.'

'He managed it well,' said her host, who was adjusting the new reel.

'Wonderful colours,' said her hostess. 'Oh, I'm so glad you dug them out. How healthy and tanned and open-necked everyone looks. And those adorable shiny natives all over the place.'

The elderly lady said, 'I liked the bit where you came out on the verandah in your shorts carrying the gun.'

'Ready?' said Sybil's host. The new reel was fixed. 'Put out the lights,' he said.

It was the stoep again. Through the french windows came a dark girl in shorts followed by a frisky young Alsatian.

'Lovely dog,' commented Sybil's host. 'He seems to be asking Sybil for a game.'

'That is someone else,' Sybil said very quickly.

'The girl there, with the dog?'

'Yes, of course. Don't you see me walking across the lawn by the trees?'

'Oh, of course, of course. She did look like you, Sybil, that girl with the dog. Wasn't she like Sybil? I mean, just as she came out on the verandah.'

'Yes, *I* thought it was Sybil for a moment until I saw Sybil in the background. But you can see the difference now. See, as she turns round. That girl isn't really like Sybil, it must be the shorts.'

'There was a slight resemblance between us,' Sybil remarked.

The projector purred on.

'Look, there's a little girl rather like you, Sybil.' Sybil, walking between her mother and father, one hand in each, had already craned round. The other child, likewise being walked along, had looked back too.

The other child wore a black velour hat turned up all round, a fawn coat of covert-coating, and at her neck a narrow white ermine tie. She wore white silk gloves. Sybil was dressed identically, and though this in itself was nothing to marvel at, since numerous small girls wore this ensemble when they were walked out in the parks and public gardens of cathedral towns in 1923, it did fortify the striking resemblance in features, build, and height, between the two children. Sybil suddenly felt she was walking past her own reflection in the long looking-glass. There was her peak chin, her black bobbed hair under her hat, with its fringe almost touching her eyebrows. Her wide-spaced eyes, her nose very small like a cat's. 'Stop staring, Sybil,' whispered her mother. Sybil had time to snatch the gleam of white socks and black patent leather button shoes. Her own socks were white but her shoes were brown, with laces. At first she felt this one discrepancy was wrong, in the sense that it was wrong to step on one of the cracks in the pavement. Then she felt it was right that there should be a difference.

'The Colemans,' Sybil's mother remarked to her father. 'They keep that hotel at Hillend. The child must be about Sybil's age. Very alike, aren't they? And I suppose,' she continued for Sybil's benefit, 'she's a good little girl like Sybil.' Quick-witted Sybil thought poorly of the last remark with its subtle counsel of perfection.

On other occasions, too, they passed the Coleman child

on a Sunday walk. In summer time the children wore panama hats and tussore silk frocks discreetly adorned with drawn-thread work. Sometimes the Coleman child was accompanied by a young maidservant in grey dress and black stockings. Sybil noted this one difference between her own entourage and the other girl's. 'Don't turn round and stare,' whispered her mother.

It was not till she went to school that she found Désirée Coleman to be a year older than herself. Désirée was in a higher class but sometimes, when the whole school was assembled on the lawn or in the gym, Sybil would be, for a few moments, mistaken for Désirée. In the late warm spring the classes sat in separate groups under the plane trees until, as by simultaneous instinct, the teachers would indicate time for break. The groups would mingle, and 'Sybil, dear, your shoe-lace,' a teacher might call out; and then, as Sybil regarded her neat-laced shoes, 'Oh no, not Sybil, I mean Désirée.' In the percussion band Sybil banged her triangle triumphantly when the teacher declared, '*Much* better than yesterday, Sybil.' But she added, 'I mean Désirée.'

Only the grown-ups mistook one child for another at odd moments. None of her small companions made this mistake. After the school concert Sybil's mother said, 'For a second I thought you were Désirée in the choir. It's strange you are so alike. I'm not a bit like Mrs Coleman and your daddy doesn't resemble *him* in the least.'

Sybil found Désirée unsatisfactory as a playmate. Sybil was precocious, her brain was like a blade. She had discovered that dull children were apt to be spiteful. Désirée would sit innocently cross-legged beside you at a party, watching the conjurer, then suddenly, for no apparent reason, jab at you viciously with her elbow.

By the time Sybil was eight and Désirée nine it was seldom that anyone, even strangers and new teachers, mixed them up. Sybil's nose became more sharp and pronounced while Désirée's seemed to sink into her plump cheeks like a painted-on nose. Only on a few occasions, and only on dark winter afternoons between the last of three o'clock daylight and the coming on of lights all over the school, was Sybil mistaken for Désirée.

Between Sybil's ninth year and her tenth Désirée's family came to live in her square. The residents' children were taken to the gardens of the square after school by mothers and nursemaids, and were bidden to play with each other nicely. Sybil regarded the intrusion of Désirée sulkily, and said she preferred her book. She cheered up, however, when a few weeks later the Dobell boys came to live in the square. The two Dobells had dusky-rose skins and fine dark eyes. It appeared the father was half Indian.

How Sybil adored the Dobells! They were a new type of playmate in her experience, so jumping and agile, and yet so gentle, so unusually courteous. Their dark skins were never dirty, a fact which Sybil obscurely approved. She did not then mind Désirée joining in their games; the Dobell boys were a kind of charm against despair, for they did not understand stupidity and so did not notice Désirée's.

The girl lacked mental stamina, could not keep up an imaginative game for long, was shrill and apt to kick her playmates unaccountably and on the sly; the Dobells reacted to this with a simple resignation. Perhaps the lack of opposition was the reason that Désirée continually shot Sybil dead, contrary to the rules, whenever she felt like it.

Sybil resented with the utmost passion the repeated daily massacre of herself before the time was ripe. It was useless for Jon Dobell to explain, 'Not yet, Désirée. Wait, wait, Désirée. She's not to be shot down yet. She hasn't crossed the bridge yet, and you can't shoot her from there, any-way – there's a big boulder between you and her. You have to creep round it, and Hugh has a shot at you first, and he thinks he's got you, but only your hat. And . . .'

It was no use. Each day before the game started the four sat in conference on the short dry prickly grass. The proceedings were agreed. The game was on. 'Got it all clear, Désirée?' 'Yes,' she said, every day. Désirée shouted and got herself excited, she made foolish sounds even when supposed to be stalking the bandits through the silent forest. A few high screams and then, 'Bang-bang,' she yelled, aiming at Sybil, 'you're dead.' Sybil obediently rolled over, protesting none the less that the game had only begun, while the Dobells sighed, 'Oh, *Désirée!*'

Sybil vowed to herself each night, I will do the same to her. Next time – tomorrow if it isn't raining – I will bang-bang her before she has a chance to hang her panama on the bough as a decoy. I will say bang-bang on her out of turn, and I will do her dead before her time.

But on no succeeding tomorrow did Sybil bring herself to do this. Her pride before the Dobells was more valuable than the success of the game. Instead, with her cleverness, Sybil set herself to avoid Désirée's range for as long as possible. She dodged behind the laurels and threw out a running commentary as if to a mental defective, such as, 'I'm in disguise, all in green, and no one can see me among the trees.' But still Désirée saw her. Désirée's eyes insisted on penetrating solid mountains. 'I'm half a mile away from everyone,' Sybil cried as Désirée's gun swivelled relentlessly upon her.

I shall refuse to be dead, Sybil promised herself. I'll break the rule. If it doesn't count with her why should it count with me? I won't roll over any more when she bangs you're dead to me. Next time, tomorrow if it isn't raining . . .

But Sybil simply did roll over. When Jon and Hugh Dobell called out to her that Désirée's bang-bang did not count she started hopefully to resurrect herself; but 'It does count, it *does*. That's the rule,' Désirée counter-screeched. And Sybil dropped back flat, knowing utterly that this was final.

And so the girl continued to deal premature death to Sybil, losing her head, but never so much that she aimed at one of the boys. For some reason which Sybil did not consider until she was years and years older, it was always herself who had to die.

One day, when Désirée was late in arriving for play, Sybil put it to the boys that Désirée should be left out of the game in future. 'She only spoils it.'

'But,' said Jon, 'you need four people for the game.'

'You need four,' said Hugh.

'No, you can do it with three.' As she spoke she was inventing the game with three. She explained to them what was in her mind's eye. But neither boy could grasp the idea, having got used to Bandits and Riders with two on each side. 'I am the lone Rider, you see,' said Sybil. 'Or,' she wheedled, 'the cherry tree can be a Rider.' She was talking to stone, inoffensive but uncomprehending. All at once she realized, without articulating the idea, that her intelligence was superior to theirs, and she felt lonely.

'Could we play rounders instead?' ventured Jon.

Sybil brought a book every day after that, and sat reading beside her mother, who was glad, on the whole, that Sybil had grown tired of rowdy games.

'They were preparing,' said Sybil, 'to go on a shoot.'

Sybil's host was changing the reel.

'I get quite a new vision of Sybil,' said her hostess, 'seeing her in such a . . . such a *social* environment. Were any of these people intellectuals, Sybil?'

'No, but lots of poets.'

'Oh, *no*. Did they all write poetry?'

'Quite a lot of them,' said Sybil, 'did.'

13

'Who *were* they all? Who was that blond fellow who was standing by the van with you?

'He was the manager of the estate. They grew passion-fruit and manufactured the juice.'

'Passion-fruit – how killing. Did *he* write poetry?'

'Oh, yes.'

'And who was the girl, the one I thought was you?'

'Oh, I had known her as a child and we met again in the Colony. The short man was her husband.'

'And were you all off on safari that morning? I simply can't imagine you shooting anything, Sybil, somehow.'

'On this occasion,' said Sybil, 'I didn't go. I just held the gun for effect.'

Everyone laughed.

'Do you still keep up with these people? I've heard that colonials are great letter-writers, it keeps them in touch with – '

'No.' And she added, 'Three of them are dead. The girl and her husband, and the fair fellow.'

'Really? What happened to them? Don't tell me *they* were mixed up in shooting affairs.'

'They were mixed up in shooting affairs,' said Sybil.

'Oh, these colonials,' said the elderly woman, 'and their shooting affairs!'

'Number three,' said Sybil's host. 'Ready? Lights out, please.'

'Don't get eaten by lions. I say, Sybil, don't get mixed up in a shooting affair.' The party at the railway station were unaware of the noise they were making for they were inside the noise. As the time of departure drew near Donald's relatives tended to herd themselves apart while Sybil's clustered round the couple.

'Two years – it will be an interesting experience for them.'

'Mind out for the shooting affairs. Don't let Donald have a gun.'

There had been an outbreak of popular headlines about the shooting affairs in the Colony. Much had been blared forth about the effect, on the minds of young settlers, of the climate, the hard drinking, the shortage of white women. The Colony was a place where lovers shot husbands, or shot themselves, where husbands shot natives who spied through bedroom windows. Letters to *The Times* arrived belatedly from respectable colonists, refuting the scandals with sober statistics. The recent incidents, they said, did not represent the habits of the peaceable majority. The Governor told the press that everything had been highly exaggerated. By the time Sybil and Donald left for the Colony the music-hall comics had already exhausted the entertainment value of colonial shooting affairs.

'Don't make pets of snakes or crocs. Mind out for the lions. Don't forget to write.'

It was almost a surprise to them to find that shooting affairs in the Colony were not entirely a music-hall myth. They occurred in waves. For three months at a time the gun-murders and suicides were reported weekly. The old colonists with their very blue eyes sat beside their whisky bottles and remarked that another young rotter had shot himself. Then the rains would break and the shootings would cease for a long season.

Eighteen months after their marriage Donald was mauled by a lioness and died on the long stretcher journey back to the station. He was one of a party of eight. No one could really say how it happened; it was done in a flash. The natives had lost their wits, and, instead of shooting the beast, had come calling 'Ah-ah-ah,' and pointing to the spot. A few strides, shouldering the grass aside, and Donald's friends got the lioness as she reared from his body.

His friends in the archaeological team to which he

belonged urged Sybil to remain in the Colony for the remaining six months, and return to England with them. Still undecided, she went on a sight-seeing tour. But before their time was up the archaeologists had been recalled. War had been declared. Civilians were not permitted to leave the continent, and Sybil was caught, like Donald under the lioness.

She wished he had lived to enjoy a life of his own, as she intended to do. It was plain to her that they must have separated had he lived. There had been no disagreement but, thought Sybil, given another two years there would have been disagreements. Donald had shown signs of becoming a bore. By the last, the twenty-seventh, year of his life, his mind had ceased to enquire. Archaeology, that thrilling subject, had become Donald's job, merely. He began to talk as if all archaeological methods and theories had ceased to evolve on the day he obtained his degree; it was now only a matter of applying his knowledge to field-work for a limited period. Archaeological papers came out from England. The usual crank literature on roneo foolscap followed them from one postal address to another. 'Donald, aren't you going to look through them?' Sybil said, as the journals and papers piled up. 'No, really, I don't see it's necessary.' It was not necessary because his future was fixed; two years in the field and then a lectureship. If it were my subject, she thought, these papers would be necessary to me. Even the crackpot ones, rightly read, would be, to me, enlarging.

Sybil lay in bed in the mornings reading the translation of Kierkegaard's *Journals*, newly arrived from England in their first, revelatory month of publication. She felt like a desert which had not realized its own aridity till the rain began to fall upon it. When Donald came home in the late afternoons she had less and less to say to him.

'There has been another shooting affair,' Donald said,

'across the valley. The chap came home unexpectedly and found his wife with another man. He shot them both.'

'In this place, one is never far from the jungle,' Sybil said.

'What are you talking about? We are eight hundred miles from the jungle.'

When he had gone on his first big shoot, eight hundred miles away in the jungle, she had reflected, there is no sign of a living mind in him, it is like a landed fish which has ceased to palpitate. But, she thought, another woman would never notice it. Other women do not wish to be married to a Mind. Yet I do, she thought, and I am a freak and should not have married. In fact I am not the marrying type. Perhaps that is why he does not explore my personality, any more than he reads the journals. It might make him think, and that would be hurtful.

After his death she wished he had lived to enjoy a life of his own, whatever that might have been. She took a job in a private school for girls and cultivated a few friends for diversion until the war should be over. Charming friends need not possess minds.

Their motor launch was rocking up the Zambesi. Sybil was leaning over the rail mouthing something to a startled native in a canoe. Now Sybil was pointing across the river.

'I think I was asking him,' Sybil commented to her friends in the darkness, 'about the hippo. There was a school of hippo some distance away, and we wanted to see them better. But the native said we shouldn't go too near – that's why he's looking so frightened – because the hippo often upset a boat, and then the crocs quickly slither into the water. There, look! We got a long shot of the hippo – those bumps in the water, like submarines, those are the snouts of hippo.'

The film rocked with the boat as it proceeded up the river. The screen went white.

'Something's happened,' said Sybil's hostess.

'Put on the light,' said Sybil's host. He fiddled with the projector and a young man, their lodger from upstairs, went to help him.

'I loved those tiny monkeys on the island,' said her hostess. 'Do hurry, Ted. What's gone wrong?'

'Shut up a minute,' he said.

'Sybil, you know you haven't changed much since you were a girl.'

'Thank you, Ella.' I haven't changed at all so far as I still think charming friends need not possess minds.

'I expect this will revive your memories, Sybil. The details, I mean. One is bound to forget so much.'

'Oh yes,' Sybil said, and she added, 'but I recall quite a lot of details, you know.'

'Do you *really*, Sybil?'

I wish, she thought, they wouldn't cling to my least word.

The young man turned from the projector with several feet of the film-strip looped between his widespread hands. 'Is the fair chap your husband, Mrs Greeves?' he said to Sybil.

'Sybil lost her husband very early on,' her hostess informed him in a low and sacred voice.

'Oh, I *am* sorry.'

Sybil's hostess replenished the drinks of her three guests. Her host turned from the projector, finished his drink, and passed his glass to be refilled, all in one movement. Everything they do seems large and important, thought Sybil, but I must not let it be so. We are only looking at old films.

She overheard a sibilant 'Whish-sh-sh?' from the elderly woman in which she discerned, 'Who is she?'

'Sybil Greeves,' her hostess breathed back, 'a distant cousin of Ted's through marriage.'

18

'Oh yes?' The low tones were puzzled as if all had not been explained.

'She's quite famous, of course.'

'Oh, I didn't know that.'

'Very few people know it,' said Sybil's hostess with a little arrogance.

'O.K.,' said Ted, 'lights out.'

'I must say,' said his wife, 'the colours are marvellous.'

All the time she was in the Colony Sybil longed for the inexplicable colourings of her native land. The flamboyants were too rowdy, the birds, the native women with their heads bound in cloth of piercing pink, their blinding black skin and white teeth, the baskets full of bright tough flowers or oranges on their heads, the sight of which everyone else admired ('How I wish I could paint all this!') distressed Sybil, it bored her.

She rented a house, sharing it with a girl whose husband was fighting in the north. She was twenty-two. To safe-guard her privacy absolutely, she had a plywood partition put up in the sitting-room, for it was another ten years before she had learnt those arts of leading a double life and listening to people ambiguously, which enabled her to mix without losing identity, and to listen without boredom.

On the other side of the partition Ariadne Lewis decor-ously entertained her friends, most of whom were men on leave. On a few occasions Sybil attended these parties, working herself, as in a frenzy of self-discipline, into a state of carnal excitement over the men. She managed to do this only by an effortful sealing-off of all her critical faculties except those which assessed a good male voice and appear-ance. The hangovers were frightful.

The scarcity of white girls made it easy for any one of them to keep a number of men in perpetual attendance. Ariadne had many boy-friends but no love affairs. Sybil had three affairs in the space of two years, to put herself to the test. They started at private dances, in the magnolia-filled gardens that smelt like a scent factory, under the Milky Way which looked like an overcrowded jeweller's window. The affairs ended when she succumbed to one of her attacks of tropical 'flu, and lay in a twilight of the senses on a bed which had been set on the stone stoep and overhung with a white mosquito net like something bridal. With damp shaky hands she would write a final letter to the man and give it to her half-caste maid to post. He would telephone next morning, and would be put off by the house boy, who was quite intelligent.

For some years she had been thinking she was not much inclined towards sex. After the third affair, this dawned and rose within her as a whole realization, as if in the past, when she had told herself, 'I am not predominantly a sexual being,' or 'I'm rather a frigid freak, I suppose,' these were the sayings of an illiterate, never quite rational and known until now, but after the third affair the notion was so intensely conceived as to be almost new. It appalled her. She lay on the shady stoep, her fever subsiding, and examined her relations with men. She thought, what if I married again? She shivered under the hot sheet. Can it be, she thought, that I have a suppressed tendency towards women? She lay still and let the idea probe round in imagination. She surveyed, with a stony inward eye, all the women she had known, prim little academicians with cream peter-pan collars on their dresses, large dominant women, a number of beauties, conventional nitwits like Ariadne. No, really, she thought; neither men nor women. It is a not caring for sexual relations. It is not merely a lack of pleasure in sex, it is dislike of the excitement. And it is not merely dislike, it is worse, it is boredom.

She felt a lonely emotion near to guilt. The three love affairs took on heroic aspects in her mind. They were an attempt, thought Sybil, to do the normal thing. Perhaps I may try again. Perhaps, if I should meet the right man . . . But at the idea 'right man' she felt a sense of intolerable desolation and could not stop shivering. She raised the mosquito net and reached for the lemon juice, splashing it jerkily into the glass. She sipped. The juice had grown warm and had been made too sweet, but she let it linger on her sore throat and peered through the net at the backs of houses and the yellow veldt beyond them.

Ariadne said one morning, 'I met a girl last night, it was funny. I thought it was you at first and called over to her. But she wasn't really like you close up, it was just an impression. As a matter of fact, she knows you. I've asked her to tea. I forget her name.'

'I don't,' said Sybil.

But when Désirée arrived they greeted each other with exaggerated warmth, wholly felt at the time, as acquaintances dó when they meet in another hemisphere. Sybil had last seen Désirée at a dance in Hampstead, and there had merely said, 'Oh, hallo.'

'We were at our first school together,' Désirée explained to Ariadne, still holding Sybil's hand.

Already Sybil wished to withdraw. 'It's strange,' she remarked, 'how, sooner or later, everyone in the Colony meets someone they have known, or their parents knew, at home.'

Désirée and her husband, Barry Weston, were settled in a remote part of the Colony. Sybil had heard of Weston, unaware that Désirée was his wife. He was much talked of as an enterprising planter. Some years ago he had got the idea of manufacturing passion-fruit juice, had planted orchards and set up a factory. The business was now expanding wonderfully. Barry Weston also wrote poetry, a volume of which, entitled *Home Thoughts*, he had published and sold with great success within the confines of the Colony. His first wife had died of blackwater fever. On one of his visits to England he had met and married Désirée, who was twelve years his junior.

'You *must* come and see us,' said Désirée to Sybil; and to Ariadne she explained again, 'We were at our first little private school together.' And she said, 'Oh, Sybil, do you remember Trotsky? Do you remember Minnie Mouse, what a hell of a life we gave her? I shall never forget that day when . . .'

The school where Sybil taught was shortly to break up for holidays; Ariadne was to visit her husband in Cairo at that time. Sybil promised a visit to the Westons. When Désirée, beautifully dressed in linen suiting, had departed, Ariadne said, 'I'm so glad you're going to stay with them. I hated the thought of your being all alone for the next few weeks.'

'Do you know,' Sybil said, 'I don't think I shall go to stay with them after all. I'll make an excuse.'

'Oh, why not? Oh, Sybil, it's such a lovely place, and it will be fun for you. He's a poet, too.' Sybil could sense exasperation, could hear Ariadne telling her friends, 'There's something wrong with Sybil. You never know a person till you live with them. Now Sybil will say one thing one minute, and the next . . . Something wrong with her sex-life, perhaps . . . odd . . .'

At home, thought Sybil, it would not be such a slur. Her final appeal for a permit to travel to England had just been dismissed. The environment mauled her weakness. 'I think I'm going to have a cold,' she said, shivering.

'Go straight to bed, dear.' Ariadne called for black Elijah and bade him prepare some lemon juice. But the cold did not materialize.

She returned with 'flu, however, from her first visit to the Westons. Her 1936 Ford V8 had broken down on the road and she had waited three chilly hours before another car had appeared.

'You must get a decent car,' said the chemist's wife, who came to console her. 'These old crocks simply won't stand up to the roads out here.'

Sybil shivered and held her peace. Nevertheless, she returned to the Westons at mid-term.

Désirée's invitations were pressing, almost desperate. Again and again Sybil went in obedience to them. The Westons were a magnetic field.

There was a routine attached to her arrival. The elegant wicker chair was always set for her in the same position on the stoep. The same cushions, it seemed, were always piled in exactly the same way.

'What will you drink, Sybil? Are you comfy there, Sybil? We're going to give you a wonderful time, Sybil.' She was their little orphan, she supposed. She sat, with very dark glasses, contemplating the couple. 'We've planned – haven't we, Barry? – a surprise for you, Sybil.' 'We've planned – haven't we, Désirée? – a marvellous trip . . . a croc hunt . . . hippo . . .'

Sybil sips her gin and lime. Facing her on the wicker sofa, Désirée and her husband sit side by side. They gaze at Sybil affectionately. 'Take off your smoked glasses, Sybil, the sun's nearly gone.' Sybil takes them off. The couple hold hands. They peck kisses at each other, and presently, outrageously, they are entwined in a long erotic embrace in the course of which Barry one or twice regards Sybil from the corner of his eye. Barry disengages himself and sits with his arm about his wife; she snuggles up to him. Why, thinks Sybil, is this performance being staged? 'Sybil is shocked,' Barry remarks. She sips her drink, and reflects that a public display between man and wife somehow is more shocking than are courting couples in parks and doorways. 'We're

23

very much in love with each other,' Barry explains, squeezing his wife. And Sybil wonders what is wrong with their marriage since obviously something is wrong. The couple kiss again. Am I dreaming this? Sybil asks herself.

Even on her first visit Sybil knew definitely there was something wrong with the marriage. She thought of herself, at first, as an objective observer, and was even amused when she understood they had chosen her to be their sort of Victim of Expiation. On occasions when other guests were present she noted that the love scenes did not take place. Instead, the couple tended to snub Sybil before their friends. 'Poor little Sybil, she lives all alone and is a teacher, and hasn't many friends. We have her here to stay as often as possible.' The people would look uneasily at Sybil, and would smile. 'But you must have *heaps* of friends,' they would say politely. Sybil came to realize she was an object of the Westons' resentment, and that, nevertheless, they found her indispensable.

Ariadne returned from Cairo. 'You always looked washed out when you've been staying at the Westons,' she told Sybil eventually. 'I suppose it's due to the late parties and lots of drinks.'

'I suppose so.'

Désirée wrote continually. 'Do come, Barry needs you. He needs your advice about some sonnets.' Sybil tore up these letters quickly, but usually went. Not because her discomfort was necessary to their wellbeing, but because it was somehow necessary to her own. The act of visiting the Westons alleviated her sense of guilt.

I believe, she thought, they must discern my abnormality. How could they have guessed? She was always cautious when they dropped questions about her private life. But one's closest secrets have a subtle way of communicating themselves to the resentful vigilance of opposite types. I do believe, she thought, that heart speaks unto heart, and deep calleth unto deep. But rarely in clear language. There is a misunderstanding here. They imagine their demonstrations of erotic bliss will torment my frigid soul, and so far they are right. But the reason for my pain is not envy. Really, it is boredom.

Her Ford V8 rattled across country. How bored, she thought, I am going to be by their married tableau! How pleased, exultant, they will be! These thoughts consoled her, they were an offering to the gods.

'Are you comfy, Sybil?'

She sipped her gin and lime. 'Yes, thanks.'

His pet name for Désirée was Dearie. 'Kiss me, Dearie,' he said.

'There, Baddy,' his wife said to Barry, snuggling close to him and squinting at Sybil.

'I say, Sybil,' Barry said as he smoothed down his hair, 'you ought to get married again. You're missing such a lot.'

'Yes, Sybil,' said Désirée, 'you should either marry or enter a convent, one or the other.'

'I don't see why,' Sybil said, 'I should fit into a tidy category.'

'Well, you're neither one thing nor another – is she, honeybunch?'

True enough, thought Sybil, and that is why I'm laid out on the altar of boredom.

'Or get yourself a boy-friend,' said Désirée. 'It would be good for you.'

'You're wasting your best years,' said Barry.

'Are you comfy there, Sybil? . . . We want you to enjoy yourself here. Any time you want to bring a boy-friend, we're broadminded – aren't we, Baddy?'

'Kiss me, Dearie,' he said.

Désirée took his handkerchief from his pocket and rubbed lipstick from his mouth. He jerked his head away and said to Sybil, 'Pass your glass.'

Désirée looked at her reflection in the glass of the french windows and said, 'Sybil's too intellectual, that's her trouble.' She patted her hair, then looked at Sybil with an old childish enmity.

After dinner Barry would read his poems. Usually, he said, 'I'm not going to be an egotist tonight. I'm not going to read my poems.' And usually Désirée would cry, 'Oh do, Barry, do.' Always, eventually, he did. 'Marvellous,' Désirée would comment, 'wonderful.' By the third night of her visits, the farcical aspect of it all would lose its fascination for Sybil, and boredom would fill her near to bursting point, like gas in a balloon. To relieve the strain, she would sigh deeply from time to time. Barry was too engrossed in his own voice to notice this, but Désirée was watching. At first Sybil worded her comments tactfully. 'I think you should devote more of your time to your verses,' she said. And, since he looked puzzled, added, 'You owe it to poetry if you write it.'

'Nonsense,' said Désirée, 'he often writes a marvellous sonnet before shaving in the morning.'

'Sybil may be right,' said Barry. 'I owe poetry all the time I can give.'

'Are you tired, Sybil?' said Désirée. 'Why are you sighing like that; are you all right?'

Later, Sybil gave up the struggle and wearily said, 'Very good,' or 'Nice rhythm' after each poem. And even the guilt of condoning Désirée's 'marvellous . . . wonderful' was less than the guilt of her isolated mind. She did not know then that the price of allowing false opinions was the gradual loss of one's capacity for forming true ones.

Not every morning, but at least twice during each visit Sybil would wake to hear the row in progress. The nanny, who brought her early tea, made large eyes and tiptoed warily. Sybil would have her bath, splashing a lot to drown the noise of the quarrel. Downstairs, the battle of voices descended, filled every room and corridor. When, on the worst occasions, the sound of shattering glass broke through the storm, Sybil would know that Barry was smashing up Désirée's dressing table; and would wonder how Désirée always managed to replace her crystal bowls, since goods of that type were now scarce, and why she bothered to do so. Sybil would always find the two girls of Barry's former marriage standing side by side on the lawn frankly gazing up at the violent bedroom window. The nanny would cart off Désirée's baby for a far-away walk. Sybil would likewise disappear for the morning.

The first time this happened, Désirée told her later, 'I'm afraid you unsettle Barry.'

'What do you mean?' said Sybil.

Désirée dabbed her watery eyes and blew her nose. 'Well, of *course*, it stands to reason, Sybil, you're out to attract Barry. And he's only a man. I know you do it *unconsciously*, but . . .'

'I can't stand this sort of thing. I shall leave right away,' Sybil said.

'No, Sybil, no. Don't make a *thing* of it. Barry needs you. You're the only person in the Colony who can really talk to him about his poetry.'

'Understand,' said Sybil on that first occasion, 'I am not at all interested in your husband. I think he's an all-round third-rater. That is my opinion.'

Désirée looked savage. 'Barry,' she shouted, 'has made a fortune out of passion-fruit juice in eight years. He has sold four thousand copies of *Home Thoughts* on his own initiative.'

It was like a game for three players. According to the rules, she was to be in love, unconsciously, with Barry, and tortured by the contemplation of Désirée's married bliss. She felt too old to join in, just at that moment.

Barry came to her room while she was packing. 'Don't

go,' he said. 'We need you. And after all, we are only human. What's a row? These quarrels only happen in the best marriages. And I can't for the life of me think how it started.'

'What a beautiful house. What a magnificent estate,' said Sybil's hostess.

'Yes,' said Sybil, 'it was the grandest in the Colony.'

'Were the owners frightfully grand?'

'Well, they were rich, of course.'

'I can see that. What a beautiful interior. I adore those lovely old oil lamps. I suppose you didn't have electricity?'

'Yes, there was electric light in all the rooms. But my friends preferred the oil-lamp tradition for the dining-room. You see, it was a copy of an old Dutch house.'

'Absolutely charming.'

The reel came to an end. The lights went up and everyone shifted in their chairs.

'What were those large red flowers?' said the elderly lady.

'Flamboyants.'

'Magnificent,' said her hostess. 'Don't you miss the colours, Sybil?'

'No, I don't actually. There was too much of it for me.'

'You didn't care for the bright colours?' said the young man, leaning forward eagerly.

Sybil smiled at him.

'I liked the bit where those little lizards were playing among the stones. That was an excellent shot,' said her host. He was adjusting the last spool.

'I rather *liked* that handsome blond fellow,' said her hostess, as if the point had been in debate. 'Was he the passion-fruiter?'

'He was the manager,' said Sybil.

'Oh yes, you told me. He was in a shooting affair, did you say?'

28

'Yes, it was unfortunate.'

'Poor young man. It sounds quite a dangerous place. I suppose the sun and everything . . .'

'It was dangerous for some people. It depended.'

'The blacks look happy enough. Did you have any trouble with them in those days?'

'No,' said Sybil, 'only with the whites.'

Everyone laughed.

'Right,' said her host. 'Lights out, please.'

Sybil soon perceived the real cause of the Westons' quarrels. It differed from their explanations: they were both, they said, so much in love, so jealous of each other's relations with the opposite sex.

'Barry was furious,' said Désirée one day, ' – weren't you, Barry? – because I smiled, merely smiled, at Carter.'

'I'll have it out with Carter,' muttered Barry. 'He's always hanging round Désirée.'

David Carter was their manager. Sybil was so foolish as once to say, 'Oh surely David wouldn't – '

'Oh wouldn't he?' said Désirée.

'Oh wouldn't he?' said Barry.

Possibly they did not themselves know the real cause of their quarrels. These occurred on mornings when Barry had decided to lounge in bed and write poetry. Désirée, anxious that the passion-fruit business should continue to expand, longed for him to be at his office in the factory at eight o'clock each morning, by which time all other enterprising men in the Colony were at work. But Barry spoke more and more of retiring and devoting his time to his poems. When he lay abed, pen in hand, worrying a sonnet, Désirée would sulk and bang doors. The household knew that the row was on. 'Quiet! Don't you see I'm trying to think,' he would shout. '*I* suggest,' she would reply, 'you go to the library if you want to write.' It was evident that her

29

greed and his vanity, facing each other in growling anti-
pathy, were too terrible for either to face. Instead, the
names of David Carter and Sybil would fly between them,
consoling them, pepping-up and propagating the myth of
their mutual attraction.

'Rolling your eyes at Carter in the orchard. Don't think I
didn't notice.'

'Carter? That's funny. I can easily keep Carter in his
place. But while we're on the subject, what about you and
Sybil? You sat up late enough with her last night after I'd
gone to bed.'

Sometimes he not only smashed the crystal bowls, he
hurled them through the window.

In the exhausted afternoon Barry would explain, 'Désirée
was upset – weren't you, Désirée? – because of you, Sybil.
It's understandable. We shouldn't stay up late talking after
Désirée has gone to bed. You're a little devil in your way,
Sybil.'

'Oh well,' said Sybil obligingly, 'that's how it is.'

She became tired of the game. When, in the evenings,
Barry's voice boomed forth with sonorous significance as
befits a hallowed subject, she no longer thought of herself as
an objective observer. She had tired of the game because
she was now more than nominally committed to it. She
ceased to be bored by the Westons; she began to hate
them.

'What I don't understand,' said Barry, 'is why my poems
are ignored back in England. I've sold over four thousand of
the book out here. Feature articles about me have appeared
in all the papers out here; remind me to show you them. But
I can't get a single notice in London. When I send a poem
to any of the magazines I don't even get a reply.'

'They are engaged in a war,' Sybil said.

'But they still publish poetry. Poetry so-called. Utter
rubbish, all of it. You can't understand the stuff.'

'Yours is too good for them,' said Sybil. To a delicate ear her tone might have resembled the stab of a pin stuck into a waxen image.

'That's a fact, between ourselves,' said Barry. 'I shouldn't say it, but that's the answer.'

Barry was over-weight, square and dark. His face had lines, as of anxiety or stomach trouble. David Carter, when he passed, cool and fair through the house, was quite a change.

'England is finished,' said Barry. 'It's degenerate.'

'I wonder,' said Sybil, 'you have the heart to go on writing so cheerily about the English towns and country-side.' Now, now, Sybil, she thought; business is business, and the nostalgic English scene is what the colonists want. This visit must be my last. I shall not come again.

'Ah, that,' Barry was saying, 'was the England I remember. The good old country. But now, I'm afraid, it's decadent. After the war it will be no more than . . .'

Désirée would have the servants into the drawing-room every morning to give them their orders for the day. 'I believe in keeping up home standards,' said Désirée, whose parents were hotel managers. Sybil was not sure where Désirée had got the idea of herding all the domestics into her presence each morning. Perhaps it was some family-prayer assembly in her ancestral memory, or possibly it had been some hotel-staff custom which prompted her to 'have in the servants' and instruct them beyond their capacity. These half-domesticated peasants and erstwhile small-farmers stood, bare-footed and woolly-cropped, in clumsy postures on Désirée's carpet. In pidgin dialect which they largely failed to comprehend, she enunciated the duties of each one. Only Sybil and David Carter knew that the natives' name for Désirée was, translated, 'Bad Hen'. Désirée complained much about their stupidity, but she enjoyed this morning palaver as Barry relished his poetry.

'Carter writes poetry too,' said Barry with a laugh one day.

Désirée shrieked. 'Poetry! Oh, Barry, you can't call that stuff *poetry*.'

'It is frightful,' Barry said, 'but the poor fellow doesn't know it.'

'I should like to see it,' Sybil said.

'You aren't interested in Carter by any chance, Sybil?' said Désirée.

'How do you mean?'

'Personally, I mean.'

'Well, I think he's all right.'

'Be honest, Sybil,' said Barry. Sybil felt extremely irritated. He so often appealed for frankness in others, as if by right; was so dishonest with himself. 'Be honest, Sybil – you're after David Carter.'

'He's handsome,' Sybil said.

'You haven't a chance,' said Barry. 'He's mad keen on Désirée. And anyway, Sybil, you don't want a beginner.'

'You want a mature man in a good position,' said Désirée. 'The life you're living isn't natural for a girl. I've been noticing,' she said, 'you and Carter being matey together out on the farm.'

Towards the end of her stay David Carter produced his verses for Sybil to read. She thought them interesting but unpractised. She told him so, and was disappointed that he did not take this as a reasonable criticism. He was very angry. 'Of course,' she said, 'your poetry is far better than Barry's.' This failed to appease David. After a while, when she was meeting him in the town where she lived, she began to praise his poems, persuading herself that he was fairly talented.

She met him whenever he could get away. She sent

32

excuses in answer to Désirée's pressing invitations. For different reasons, both Sybil and David were anxious to keep their meetings secret from the Westons. Sybil did not want the affair mythologized and gossiped about. For David's part, he valued his job in the flourishing passion-fruit concern. He had confided to Sybil his hope, one day, to have the whole business under his control. He might even buy Barry out. 'I know far more about it than he does. He's getting more and more bound up with his poetry, and paying next to no attention to the business. I'm just waiting.' He is, Sybil remarked to herself on hearing this, a true poet all right.

David reported that the quarrels between Désirée and Barry were becoming more violent, that the possibility of Barry's resigning from business to devote his time to poetry was haunting Désirée. 'Why don't you come,' Désirée wrote, 'and talk to Barry about his poetry? Why don't you come and see us now? What have we done? Poor Sybil, all alone in the world, you ought to be married. David Carter follows me all over the place, it's most embarrassing, you know how furious Barry gets. Well, I suppose that's the cost of having a devoted husband.' Perhaps, thought Sybil, she senses that David is my lover.

One day she went down with 'flu. David turned up unexpectedly and proposed marriage. He clung to her with violent, large hands. She alone, he said, understood his ambitions, his art, himself. Within a year or two they could, together, take over the passion-fruit plantation.

'Sh-sh Ariadne will hear you.' Ariadne was out, in fact. David looked at her somewhat wildly. 'We must be married,' he said.

Sybil's affair with David Carter was over, from her point of view, almost before it had started. She had engaged in it as an act of virtue done against the grain, and for a brief time it had absolved her from the reproach of her sexlessness.

'I'm waiting for an answer.' By his tone, he seemed to suspect what the answer would be.

'Oh, David, I was just about to write to you. We really must put an end to this. As for marriage, well, I'm not cut out for it at all.'

He stooped over her bed and clung to her, 'You'll catch my 'flu,' she said. 'I'll think about it,' she said, to get rid of him.

When he had gone she wrote him her letter, sipping lemon juice to ease her throat. She noticed he had brought for her, and left on the floor of the stoep, six bottles of Weston's Passion-fruit Juice. He will soon get over the affair, she thought, he has still got his obsession with the passion-fruit business.

But in response to her letter David forced his way into the house. Sybil was alarmed. None of her previous lovers had persisted in this way.

'It's your duty to marry me.'

'Really, what next?'

'It's your duty to me as a man and a poet.' She did not like his eyes.

'As a poet,' she said, 'I think you're a third-rater.' She felt relieved to hear her own voice uttering the words.

He stiffened up in a comical melodramatic style, looking such a clean-cut settler with his golden hair and tropical suiting.

'David Carter,' wrote Désirée, 'has gone on the bottle. I think he's bats, myself. It's because I keep giving him the brush-off. Isn't it all silly? The estate will go to ruin if Barry doesn't get rid of him. Barry has sent him away on leave for a month, but if he hasn't improved on his return we shall have to make a change. When are you coming? Barry needs to talk to you.'

Sybil went the following week, urged on by her old self-despising; driving her Ford V8 against the current of pleasure, yet compelled to expiate her abnormal nature by contact with the Westons' sexuality, which she knew, none the less, would bore her.

They twisted the knife within an hour of her arrival.

'Haven't you found a man yet?' said Barry.

'You ought to try a love affair,' said Désirée. 'We've been saying – haven't we, Barry? – you ought to, Sybil. It would be good for you. It isn't healthy, the life you lead. That's why you get 'flu so often. It's psychological.'

'Come out on the lawn,' Barry had said when she first arrived. 'We've got the ciné camera out. Come and be filmed.'

Désirée said, 'Carter came back this morning.'

'Oh, is he here? I thought he was away for a month.'

'So did we. But he turned up this morning.'

'He's moping,' Barry said, 'about Désirée. She snubs him so badly.'

'He's psychological,' said Désirée.

'I love that striped awning,' said Sybil's hostess. 'It puts the finishing touch on the whole scene. How carefree you all look – don't they, Ted?'

'*That* chap looks miserable,' Ted observed. He referred to a shot of David Carter who had just ambled within range of the camera.

Everyone laughed, for David looked exceedingly grim.

'He was caught in an off-moment there,' said Sybil's hostess. 'Oh, there goes Sybil. I thought you looked a little sad just then, Sybil. There's that other girl again, and the lovely dog.'

'Was this a *typical* afternoon in the Colony?' enquired the young man.

'It was and it wasn't,' Sybil said.

Whenever they had the camera out life changed at the

Westons. Everyone, including the children, had to look very happy. The house natives were arranged to appear in the background wearing their best whites. Sometimes Barry would have everyone dancing in a ring with the children, and the natives had to clap time.

Or, as on the last occasion, he would stage an effect of gracious living. The head cook-boy, who had a good knowledge of photography, was placed at his post.

'Ready,' said Barry to the cook, 'shoot.'

Désirée came out, followed by the dog.

'Look frisky, Barker,' said Barry. The Alsatian looked frisky.

Barry put one arm round Désirée and his other arm through Sybil's that late afternoon, walking them slowly across the camera range. He chatted with amiability and with an actor's lift of the head. He would accentuate his laughter, tossing back his head. A sound track would, however, have reproduced the words, 'Smile, Sybil. Walk slowly. Look as if you're enjoying it. You'll be able to see yourself in later years, having the time of your life.'

Sybil giggled.

Just then David was seen to be securing the little lake boat between the trees. 'He must have come across the lake,' said Barry. 'I wonder if he's been drinking again?'

But David's walk was quite steady. He did not realize he was being photographed as he crossed the long lawn. He stood for a moment staring at Sybil. She said, 'Oh hallo, David.' He turned and walked aimlessly face-on towards the camera.

'Hold it a minute,' Barry called out to the cook.

The boy obeyed at the moment David realized he had been filmed.

'O.K.,' shouted Barry, when David was out of range. 'Fire ahead.'

It was then Barry said to Sybil, 'Haven't you found a

36

man yet . . .' and Désirée said, 'You ought to try a love affair . . .'

'We've made Sybil unhappy,' said Désirée.

'Oh, I'm quite happy.'

'Well, cheer up in front of the camera,' said Barry.

The sun was setting fast, the camera was folded away, and everyone had gone to change. Sybil came down and sat on the stoep outside the open french windows of the dining-room. Presently, Désirée was indoors behind her, adjusting the oil lamps which one of the house-boys had set too high. Désirée put her head round the glass door and remarked to Sybil, 'That Benjamin's a fool, I shall speak to him in the morning. He simply will not take care with these lamps. One day we'll have a real smoke-out.'

Sybil said, 'Oh, I expect they are all so used to electricity these days . . .'

'That's the trouble,' said Désirée, and turned back into the room.

Sybil was feeling disturbed by David's presence in the place. She wondered if he would come in to dinner. Thinking of his sullen staring at her on the lawn, she felt he might make a scene. She heard a gasp from the dining-room behind her.

She looked round, but in the same second it was over. A deafening crack from the pistol and Désirée crumpled up. A movement by the inner door and David held the gun to his head. Sybil screamed, and was aware of running footsteps upstairs. The gun exploded again and David's body dropped sideways.

With Barry and the natives she went round to the dining-room. Désirée was dead. David lingered a moment enough to roll his eyes in Sybil's direction as she rose from Désirée's body. He knows, thought Sybil quite lucidly, that he got the wrong woman.

*

37

'What I can't understand,' said Barry when he called on Sybil a few weeks later, 'is why he did it.'

'He was mad,' said Sybil.

'Not all that mad,' said Barry. 'And everyone thinks, of course, that there was an affair between them. That's what I can't bear.'

'Quite,' said Sybil. 'But of course he was keen on Désirée. You always said so. Those rows you used to have . . . You always made out you were jealous of David.'

'Do you know,' he said, 'I wasn't really. It was a sort of . . . a sort of . . .'

'Play-act,' said Sybil.

'Sort of. You see, there was nothing between them,' he said, 'And honestly, Carter wasn't a bit interested in Désirée. And the question is *why* he did it. I can't bear people to think . . .'

The damage to his pride, Sybil saw, outweighed his grief. The sun was setting and she rose to put on the stoep light.

'Stop!' he said. 'Turn round. My God, you did look like Désirée for a moment.'

'You're nervy,' she said, and switched on the light.

'In some ways you *do* look a little like Désirée,' he said. 'In some lights,' he said reflectively.

I must say something, thought Sybil, to blot this notion from his mind. I must make this occasion unmemorable, distasteful to him.

'At all events,' she said, 'you've still got your poetry.'

'That's the great thing,' he said, 'I've still got that. It means everything to me, a great consolation. I'm selling up the estate and joining up. The kids are going into a convent and I'm going up north. What we need is some good war poetry. There hasn't been any war poetry.'

'You'll make a better soldier,' she said, 'than a poet.'

'What do you say?'

She repeated her words fairly slowly, and with a sense of relief, almost of absolution. The season of falsity had formed a scab, soon to fall away altogether. There is no health, she thought, for me, outside of honesty.

'You've always,' he said, 'thought my poetry was wonderful.'

'I have said so,' she said, 'but it was a sort of play-act. Of course, it's only my opinion, but I think you're a third-rater poet.'

'You're upset, my dear,' he said.

He sent her the four reels of film from Cairo a month before he was killed in action. 'It will be nice in later years,' he wrote, 'for you to recall those good times we used to have.'

'It has been delightful,' said her hostess. 'You haven't changed a bit. Do you *feel* any different?'

'Well yes, I feel rather differently about everything, of course.' One learns to accept oneself.

'A hundred feet of one's past life!' said the young man. 'If they were mine, I'm sure I should be shattered. I should be calling "Lights! Lights!" like Hamlet's uncle.'

Sybil smiled at him. He looked back, suddenly solemn and shrewd.

'How tragic, those people being killed in shooting affairs,' said the elderly woman.

'The last reel was the best,' said her hostess. 'The garden was entrancing. I should like to see that one again; what about you, Ted?'

'Yes, I liked those nature-study shots. I feel I missed a lot of it,' said her husband.

'Hark at him – nature-study shots!'

'Well, those close-ups of tropical plants.'

Everyone wanted the last one again.

'How about you, Sybil?'

Am I a woman, she thought calmly, or an intellectual monster? She was so accustomed to this question within herself that it needed no answer. She said, 'Yes, I should like to see it again. It's an interesting experience.'

The Gentile Jewesses

One day a madman came into my little grandmother's shop at Watford. I say my little grandmother but 'little' refers only to her height and to the dimensions of her world by the square foot – the small shop full of varieties, her parlour behind it, and behind that the stone kitchen and the two bedrooms over her head.

'I shall murder you,' said the madman, standing with legs straddled in the door frame, holding up his dark big hands as one about to pounce and strangle. His eyes stared from a face covered with tangled eyebrows and beard.

The street was empty. My grandmother was alone in the house. For some years, from frequent hearing of the story, I believed I was standing by her side at the time, but my grandmother said no, this was long before I was born. The scene is as clear as a memory to me. The madman – truly escaped from the asylum in a great park near-by – lifted his hairy hands, cupped as for strangling. Behind him was the street, empty save for sunshine.

He said, 'I'm going to murder you.'

She folded her hands over her white apron which lay over the black apron and looked straight at him.

'Then you'll get hung,' she said.

He turned and shuffled away.

She should have said 'hanged' and I remember at one telling of the story remarking so to my grandmother. She replied that 'hung' had been good enough for the madman. I could not impress her with words, but I was so impressed by the tale that very often afterwards I said 'hung' instead of 'hanged'.

I seem to see the happening so plainly in my memory it is difficult to believe I know it only by hearsay; but indeed it happened before I was born. My grandfather was a young man then, fifteen years younger than his wife and dispossessed by his family for having married her. He was gone to arrange about seedlings when the madman had appeared.

My grandmother had married him for pure love, she had chased him and hunted him down and married him, he was so beautiful and useless. She never cared at all that she had to work and keep him all his life. She was astonishingly ugly, one was compelled to look at her. In my actual memory, late in their marriage, he would bring her a rose from the garden from time to time, and put cushions under her head and feet when she reclined on the sofa in the parlour between the hours of two and three in the afternoon. He could not scrub the counter in her shop for he did not know how to do it, but he knew about dogs and birds and gardens, and had photography for a pastime.

He said to my grandmother, 'Stand by the dahlias and I will take your likeness.'

I wished she had known how to take his likeness because he was golden-haired even in my day, with delicate features and glittering whiskers. She had a broad pug nose, she was sallow skinned with bright black eyes staring straight at the world and her dull black hair pulled back tight into a knot. She looked like a white Negress; she did not try to beautify herself except by washing her face in rain water.

She had come from Stepney. Her mother was a Gentile and her father was a Jew. She said her father was a Quack by profession and she was proud of this, because she felt all curing was done by the kindly manner of the practitioner in handing out bottles of medicine rather than by the contents. I always forced my elders to enact their stories. I said, 'Show me how he did it.'

Willingly she leaned forward in her chair and handed me an invisible bottle of medicine. She said, 'There you are, my dear, and you won't come to grief, and don't forget to keep your bowels regular.' She said, 'My father's medicine was only beetroot juice but he took pains with his manners, and he took pains with the labels, and the bottles were three-pence a gross. My father cured many an ache and pain, it was his gracious manner.'

This, too, entered my memory and I believed I had seen the glamorous Quack Doctor who was dead before I was born. I thought of him when I saw my grandfather, with his gracious manner, administering a tiny dose of medicine out of a blue bottle to one of his small coloured birds. He opened its beak with his finger and tipped in a drop. All the little garden was full of kennels, glass and sheds containing birds and flower-pots. His photographs were not quite real to look at. One day he called me Canary and made me stand by the brick wall for my likeness. The photograph made the garden look tremendous. Perhaps he was repro-ducing in his photographs the grander garden of his youth from which he was expelled avengingly upon his marriage to my grandmother long before I was born.

After his death, when my grandmother came to live with us I said to her one day,

'Are you a Gentile, Grandmother, or are you a Jewess?' I was wondering how she would be buried, according to what religion, when her time came to die.

'I am a Gentile Jewess,' she said.

All during the time she kept the shop of all sorts in Watford she had not liked the Jewish part of her origins to be known, because it was bad for business. She would have been amazed at any suggestion that this attitude was a weak one or a wrong one. To her, whatever course was sensible and good for business was good in the sight of the Almighty. She believed heartily in the Almighty. I never

43

heard her refer to God by any other title except to say, God bless you. She was a member of the Mothers' Union of the Church of England. She attended all the social functions of the Methodists, Baptists and Quakers. This was bright and agreeable as well as being good for business. She never went to church on Sundays, only for special services such as on Remembrance Day. The only time she acted against her conscience was when she attended a spiritualist meeting; this was from sheer curiosity, not business. There, a bench fell over on to her foot and she limped for a month; it was a judgment of the Almighty.

I inquired closely about spiritualism. 'They call up the dead from their repose,' she said. 'It vexes the Almighty when the dead are stirred before they are ready.'

Then she told me what happened to spiritualists after a number of years had passed over their heads. 'They run up the garden path, look back over their shoulders, give a shudder, and run back again. I dare say they see spirits.'

I took my grandmother's hand and led her out to the garden to make her show me what spiritualists did. She ran up the path splendidly with her skirts held up in her hands, looked round with sudden bright eyes, shuddered horribly, then, with skirts held higher so that her white petticoat frills flickered round her black stockings, she ran gasping back towards me.

My grandfather came out to see the fun with his sandy eyebrows raised high among the freckles. 'Stop your larks, Adelaide,' he said to my grandmother.

So my grandmother did it again, with a curdling cry, 'Ah-ah-ah'.

Rummaging in the shop, having climbed up on two empty fizz-pop crates, I found on an upper shelf some old bundles of candles wrapped in interesting-looking literature. I smoothed out the papers and read, 'Votes for Women! Why do you Oppress Women?' Another lot of candles was wrapped in a larger bill on which was printed an old-fashioned but military-looking young woman waving the Union Jack and saying, 'I'm off to join the Suffragettes.' I asked my grandmother where the papers came from, for she never threw anything away and must have had them for another purpose before wrapping up the candles before I was born. My grandfather answered for her, so far forgetting his refinement as to say, 'Mrs Spank-arse's lark'.

'Mrs Pankhurst, he means. I'm surprised at you, Tom, in front of the child.'

My grandfather was smiling away at his own joke. And so all in one afternoon I learned a new word, and the story of my grandmother's participation in the Women's Marches down Watford High Street, dressed in her best clothes, and I learned also my grandfather's opinions about these happenings. I saw, before my very eyes, my grandmother and her banner, marching in the sunshiny street with her friends, her white petticoat twinkling at her ankles as she walked. In a few years' time it was difficult for me to believe I had not stood and witnessed the march of the Watford Suffragettes moving up the High Street, with my grandmother swiftly in the van before I was born. I recalled how her shiny black straw hat gleamed in the sun.

Some Jews came to Watford and opened a bicycle shop not far from my grandmother's. She would have nothing to do with them. They were Polish immigrants. She called them Pollacks. When I asked what this meant she said, 'foreigners'. One day the mama-foreigner came to the door of her shop as I was passing and held out a bunch of grapes. She said, 'Eat'. I ran, amazed, to my grandmother who said, 'I told you that foreigners are funny.'

Amongst ourselves she boasted of her Jewish blood because it had made her so clever. I knew she was so clever that it was unnecessary for her to be beautiful. She boasted that her ancestors on her father's side crossed over the Red

Sea; the Almighty stretched forth his hands and parted the waves, and they crossed over from Egypt on to dry land. Miriam, the sister of Moses, banged her timbrel and led all the women across the Red Sea, singing a song to the Almighty. I thought of the Salvation Army girls who quite recently had marched up Watford High Street in the sunshine banging their tambourines. My grandmother had called me to the shop door to watch, and when they and their noise were dwindled away she turned from the door and clapped her hands above her head, half in the spontaneous spirit of the thing, half in mimicry. She clapped her hands. 'Alleluia!' cried my grandmother. 'Alleluia!'

'Stop your larks, Adelaide, my dear.'

Was I present at the Red Sea crossing? No, it had happened before I was born. My head was full of stories, of Greeks and Trojans, Picts and Romans, Jacobites and Redcoats, but these were definitely outside of my lifetime. It was different where my grandmother was concerned. I see her in the vanguard, leading the women in their dance of triumph, clanging the tambourine for joy and crying Alleluia with Mrs Pankhurst and Miriam the sister of Moses. The hands of the Almighty hold back the walls of the sea. My grandmother's white lace-edged petticoat flashes beneath her black skirt an inch above her boots, as it did when she demonstrated up and down the garden path what happens to spiritualists. What part of the scene I saw and what happened before I was born can be distinguished by my reason, but my reason cannot obliterate the scene or diminish it.

Great-aunts Sally and Nancy, my grandfather's sisters, had been frigidly reconciled to him at some date before I was born. I was sent to visit them every summer. They lived quietly now, a widow and a spinster of small means. They occupied themselves with altar-flowers and the vicar. I was a Gentile Jewess like my grandmother, for my father was a

46

Jew, and these great-aunts could not make it out that I did not look like a Jew as did my grandmother. They remarked on this in my presence as if I could not understand that they were discussing my looks. I said that I did look like a Jew and desperately pointed to my small feet. 'All Jews have very little feet,' I claimed. They took this for fact, being inexperienced in Jews, and admitted to each other that I possessed this Jewish characteristic.

Nancy's face was long and thin and Sally's was round. There seemed to be a lot of pincushions on tiny tables. They gave me aniseed cake and tea every summer while the clock ticked loudly in time to their silence. I looked at the yellowish-green plush upholstery which caught streaks of the sunny afternoon outside, I looked until I had absorbed its colour and texture in a total trance during the great-aunts' silences. Once when I got back to my grandmother's and looked in the glass it seemed my eyes had changed from blue to yellow-green plush.

On one of these afternoons they mentioned my father's being an engineer. I said all Jews were engineers. They were fascinated by this fact which at the time I thought was possibly true with the exception of an occasional Quack. Then Sally looked up and said, 'But the Lingens are not engineers.'

The Lingens were not Jews either, they were Gentiles of German origin, but it came to the same thing in those parts. The Lingens were not classified as foreigners by my grandmother because they did not speak in broken English, being all of a London-born generation.

The Lingen girls were the main friends of my mother's youth. There was Lottie who sang well and Flora who played the piano and Susanna who was strange. I remember a long evening in their house when Lottie and my mother sang a duet to Flora's piano playing, while Susanna loitered darkly at the door of the drawing-room with a smile

I had never seen on any face before. I could not keep my eyes off Susanna, and got into trouble for staring.

When my mother and Lottie were seventeen they hired a cab one day and went to an inn, some miles away in the country, where they drank gin. They supplied the driver with gin as well, and, forgetting that the jaunt was supposed to be a secret one, returned two hours later standing up in the cab, chanting 'Horrid little Watford. Dirty little Watford. We'll soon say good-bye to nasty little Watford.' They did not consider themselves to be village girls and were eager to be sent away to relatives elsewhere. This was soon accomplished; Lottie went to London for a space and my mother to Edinburgh. My mother told me the story of the wild return of carriage and horses up the High Street and my grandmother confirmed it, adding that the occurrence was bad for business. I can hear the clopping of hooves, and see the girls standing wobbly in the cab dressed in their spotted muslins, although I never actually saw anything but milk-carts, motor cars and buses, and girls with short skirts in the High Street, apart from such links with antiquity as fat old Benskin of Benskins' Breweries taking his morning stroll along the bright pavement, bowing as he passed to my grandmother.

'I am a Gentile Jewess.'

She was buried as a Jewess since she died in my father's house, and notices were put in the Jewish press. Simultaneously my great-aunts announced in the Watford papers that she fell asleep in Jesus.

My mother never fails to bow three times to the new moon wherever she might be at the time of first catching sight of it. I have seen her standing on a busy pavement with numerous cold rational Presbyterian eyes upon her, turning over her money, bowing regardless and chanting, 'New moon, new moon, be good to me.' In my memory this image

48

is fused with her lighting of the Sabbath candles on a Friday night, chanting a Hebrew prayer which I have since been told came out in a very strange sort of Hebrew. Still, it was her tribute and solemn observance. She said that the Israelites of the Bible and herself were one and the same because of the Jewish part of her blood, and I did not doubt this thrilling fact. I thought of her as the second Gentile Jewess after my grandmother, and myself as the third.

My mother carries everywhere in her handbag a small locket containing a picture of Christ crowned with thorns. She keeps on one table a rather fine Buddha on a lotus leaf and on another a horrible replica of the Venus de Milo. One way and another all the gods are served in my mother's household although she holds only one belief and that is in the Almighty. My father, when questioned as to what he believes, will say, 'I believe in the Blessed Almighty who made heaven and earth,' and will say no more, returning to his racing papers which contain problems proper to innocent men. To them, it was no great shock when I turned Catholic, since with Roman Catholics too, it all boils down to the Almighty in the end.

The Curtain Blown by the Breeze

It is always when a curtain at an open window flutters in the breeze that I think of that frail white curtain, a piece of fine gauze, which was drawn across the bedroom windows of Mrs Van der Merwe. I never saw the original curtains, which were so carelessly arranged as to leave a gap through which that piccanin of twelve had peeped, one night three years before, and had watched Mrs Van der Merwe suckle her child, and been caught and shot dead by Jannie, her husband. The original curtains had now been replaced by this more delicate stuff, and the husband's sentence still had five years to run, and meanwhile Mrs Van der Merwe was changing her character.

She stopped slouching; she lost the lanky, sullen look of a smallholder's wife; she cleared the old petrol cans out of the yard, and that was only a start; she became a tall lighthouse sending out kindly beams which some took for welcome instead of warnings against the rocks. She bought the best china, stopped keeping pound notes stuffed in a stocking, called herself Sonia instead of Sonji, and entertained.

This was a territory where you could not bathe in the gentlest stream but a germ from the water entered your kidneys and blighted your body for life; where you could not go for a walk before six in the evening without returning crazed by the sun; and in this remote part of the territory, largely occupied by poor whites amidst the overwhelming natural growth of natives, a young spinster could not keep a cat for a pet but it would be one day captured and pitifully shaved by the local white bachelors for fun; it was a place where the tall grass was dangerous from snakes and the floors dangerous from scorpions. The white people seized on the slightest word, Nature took the lightest footfall, with fanatical seriousness. The English nurses discovered that they could not sit next to a man at dinner and be agreeable – perhaps asking him, so as to slice up the boredom, to tell them all the story of his life – without his taking it for a great flirtation and turning up next day after breakfast for the love affair; it was a place where there was never a breath of breeze except in the season of storms and where the curtains in the windows never moved in the breeze unless a storm was to follow.

The English nurses were often advised to put in for transfers to another district.

'It's so much brighter in the north. Towns, life. Civilization, shops. Much cooler – you see, it's high up there in the north. The races.'

'You would like it in the east – those orange-planters. Everything is greener, there's a huge valley. Shooting.'

'Why did they send you nurses to this unhealthy spot? You should go to a healthy spot.'

Some of the nurses left Fort Beit. But those of us who were doing tropical diseases had to stay on, because our clinic, the largest in the Colony, was also a research centre for tropical diseases. Those of us who had to stay on used sometimes to say to each other, 'Isn't it wonderful here? Heaps of servants. Cheap drinks. Birds, beasts, flowers.'

The place was not without its strange marvels. I never got used to its travel-film colours except in the dry season when the dust made everything real. The dust was thick in the great yard behind the clinic where the natives squatted and stood about, shouting or laughing – it came to the same thing – cooking and eating, while they awaited treatment, or the results of X-rays, or the results of an X-ray of a

51

distant relative. They gave off a fierce smell and kicked up the dust. The sore eyes of the babies were always beset by flies, but the babies slept on regardless, slung on their mothers' backs, and when they woke and cried the women suckled them.

The poor whites of Fort Beit and its area had a reception room of their own inside the building, and here they ate the food they had brought, and lolled about in long silences, sometimes working up to a fight in a corner. The remainder of the society of Fort Beit did not visit the clinic.

The remainder comprised the chemist, the clergyman, the veterinary surgeon, the police and their families. These enjoyed a social life of a small and remote quality, only coming into contact with the poor white small-farmers for business purposes. They were anxious to entertain the clinic staff who mostly spent its free time elsewhere – miles and miles away, driving at week-ends to the capital, the north, or to one of the big dams on which it was possible to set up for a sailor. But sometimes the nurses and medical officers would, for a change, spend an evening in the village at the house of the chemist, the clergyman, the vet, or at the police quarters.

Into this society came Sonia Van der Merwe when her husband had been three years in prison. There was a certain slur attached to his sentence since it was generally felt he had gone too far in the heat of the moment, this sort of thing undermining the prestige of the Colony at Whitehall. But nobody held the incident against Sonia. The main difficulty she had to face in her efforts towards the company of the vet, the chemist and the clergyman was the fact that she had never yet been in their company.

The Van der Merwes' farm lay a few miles outside Fort Beit. It was one of the few farms in the district, for this was an area which had only been developed for the mines, and these had lately closed down. The Van der Merwes had lived the makeshift, toiling lives of Afrikaans settlers who had trekked up from the Union. I do not think it had ever before occurred to Sonia that her days could be spent otherwise than in rising and washing her face at the tub outside, baking bread, scrappily feeding her children, yelling at the natives, and retiring at night to her feather bed with Jannie. Her only outings had been to the Dutch Reformed gathering at Easter when the Afrikaans came in along the main street in their covered wagons and settled there for a week.

It was not till the lawyer came to arrange some affair between the farm and the Land Bank that she learned she could actually handle the fortune her father had left her, for she imagined that only the pound notes she kept stuffed in the stocking were of real spending worth; her father in his time had never spent his money on visible things, but had invested it, and Sonia thought that money paid into the bank was a sort of tribute-money to the bank people which patriarchal farmers like her father were obliged to pay under the strict ethic of the Dutch Reformed Church. She now understood her cash value, and felt fiercely against her husband for failing to reveal it to her. She wrote a letter to him, which was a difficult course. I saw the final draft, about which she called a conference of nurses from the clinic. We were wicked enough to let it go, but in fact I don't think we gave it much thought. I recall that on this occasion we talked far into the night about her possibilities – her tennis court, her two bathrooms, her black-and-white bedroom – all of which were as yet only a glimmer at the end of a tunnel. In any case, I do not think we could have succeeded in changing her mind about the letter which subsequently enjoyed a few inches in the local press as part of Jannie's evidence. It was as follows:

Dear Jannie there is going to be some changes I found out what pa left is cash to spend I only got to sine my name do you think I like to go on like this work work work counting the mealies in the field By God like poor whites when did I get a dress you did not say a word that is your shame and you have landed in jale with your bad temper you shoud of amed at the legs. Mr Little came here to bring the papers to sine he said you get good cooking in jale the kids are well but Hannah got a bite but I will take them away from there now and send them to the convent and pay money. Your Loving Wife, S. Van der Merwe

There must have been many occasions on which I lay on my bed on summer afternoons in Worcestershire, because at that time I was convalescent. My schooldays had come to an end. My training as a radio-therapist was not to begin till the autumn.

I do not know how many afternoons I lay on my bed listening to a litany of tennis noises from where my two brothers played on the court a little to the right below my window. Sometimes, to tell me it was time to get up, my elder brother Richard would send a tennis ball through the open window. The net curtain would stir and part very suddenly and somewhere in the room the ball would thud and then roll. I always thought one day he would break the glass of the window, or that he would land the ball on my face or break something in the room, but he never did. Perhaps my memory exaggerates the number of these occasions and really they only occurred once or twice.

But I am sure the curtains must have moved in the breeze as I lay taking in the calls and the to and fro of tennis on those unconcerned afternoons, and I suppose the sight was a pleasurable one. That a slight movement of the curtains should be the sign of a summer breeze seems somewhere near to truth, for to me truth has airy properties with buoyant and lyrical effects; and when anything drastic starts up from some light cause it only proves to me that something false has got into the world.

I do not actually remember the curtains of my room being touched by the summer wind although I am sure they were; whenever I try to bring to mind this detail of the afternoon sensations it disappears, and I have knowledge of the image only as one who has swallowed some fruit of the Tree of Knowledge – its memory is usurped by the window of Mrs Van der Merwe's house and by the curtains disturbed, in the rainy season, by a trifling wind, unreasonably meaning a storm.

Sometimes, on those restful afternoons, I was anxious. There was some doubt about my acceptance for training as a radio-therapist because of my interrupted schooling. One day the letter of acceptance came by the late post. I read the letter with relief and delight, and at that same moment decided to turn down the offer. It was enough that I had received it. I am given to this sort of thing, and the reason that I am drawn to moderate and tranquil motives is that I lack them. I decided instead to become a hospital nurse and later to follow my brother Richard, who was then a medical student, to Africa, and specialize, with him, in tropical diseases.

It was about a year after my arrival at Fort Beit that I came across Sonji Van der Merwe and, together with the other nurses, read the letter which was about to be sent to her husband four hundred miles away in the Colony's prison. She posted the letter ritualistically the next afternoon, putting on her church-going gloves to do so. She did not expect, nor did she receive, a reply. Three weeks later she started calling herself Sonia.

Our visits to the farm began to take the place of evenings spent at the vet's, the chemist's and the clergyman's, to whose society Sonia now had good hopes of access. And every time we turned up something new had taken place. Sonia knew, or discovered as if by bush-telegraph, where to begin. She did not yet know how to travel by train and would have been afraid to make any excursion by herself far from the area, but through one nurse or another she obtained furnishings from the Union, catalogues, books about interior decoration and fashion magazines. Travel-stained furniture vans began to arrive at her bidding and our instigation. Her first move, however, was to join the Church of England, abandoning the Dutch Reformed per-suasion of her forefathers; we had to hand it to her that she had thought this up for herself.

We egged her on from week to week. We taught her how not to be mean with her drinks, for she had ordered an exotic supply. At first she had locked the bottles in the pantry and poured them into glasses in the kitchen and watered them before getting the house-boy to serve them to her guests. We stopped all that. A contractor already had the extensions to the house in hand, and the rooms were being decorated and furnished one by one. It was I who had told her to have two bathrooms, not merely one, installed. She took time getting used to the indoor lavatories and we had to keep reminding her to pull the chain. One of us brought back from the capital a book of etiquette which was twenty-eight years old but which she read assiduously, following the words with her forefinger. I think it was I who had suggested the black-and-white bedroom, being a bit drunk at the time, and now it was a wonder to see it taking shape; it was done within a month – she had managed to obtain black wallpaper, and to put it up, although wall-paper was a thing unheard of in the Colony and she was warned by everyone that it would never stick to the walls. There was in this bedroom a white carpet and a chaise-longue covered with black-and-white candy-striped satin. It was less than a year before she got round to adding the Beardsley reproductions, but by that time she was entertaining, and had the benefit of the vet's counsel, he having once been a young man in London.

She told us one day – lying on the chaise-longue and looking very dramatic with her lanky hair newly piled up and her black chiffon dressing-gown – the story of the piccanin, which we already knew:

'It was through that window he was looking. Yere I was sitting yere on the bed feeding the baby and I look up at the window and so help me God it was a blerry nig standing outside with his face at the window. You should of heard me scream. So Jannie got the gun and caught the pic and I hear the bang. So he went too far in his blerry temper so what can you expect? Now I won't have no more trouble from them boys. That's the very window, I was careless to leave the curtain aside. So we show them what's what and we get a new set of boys. We didn't have no boys on the farm, they all run away.'

There was a slight warm breeze floating in little gusts through the window. 'We'd better be getting back,' said one of the girls. 'There's going to be a storm.'

A storm in the Colony was such that before it broke the whole place was spasmodic like an exposed nerve, and after it was over the body of the world from horizon to horizon moved in a slow daze back into its place. Before it broke there was the little wind, then a pearly light, then an earthen smell; the birds screamed and suddenly stopped, and the insects disappeared. Afterwards the flying ants wriggled in a drugged condition out of the cracks in the walls, found their wings, and flew off in crazy directions, the more extreme colours of the storm faded out of the sky in a defeated sort of way, and the furniture felt clammy from the ordeal. One day I was caught at Sonia's house when a storm broke. This was when she had already settled in to her status, and the extensions to the house were completed, and the furniture all in place. Night fell soon after the storm was over, and we sat in her very Europeanized drawing-room – for she had done away with the stoep – sipping pink gins; the drinks were served by a native with huge ape-like hands clutching the tray, his hands emerging from the cuffs of the green-and-white uniform which had lately glared in the light of the storm. Sonia kept saying, 'I feel I've made a corner of civilization for myself in doing up this house.' It was a version of one of the clergyman's chance compliments on one of his visits; she had seized on it as a verity, and made it known to all her visitors. 'I feel I must live up to it, man,' she said. I was always amazed at her rapid acquisition of new words and highly useful sayings.

Outside, the night sounds were coming back. One could hear the beasts finding each other again by their calls whenever Sonia stopped talking, and even further in the distance, the drum business, with news of which kraals had been swamped and wrecked, or perhaps no news, for all we understood of their purpose. Just outside the window there was an occasional squelch of bare feet on the wet gravel drive which Sonia had constructed. She rose and adjusted the light window curtains, then drew the big ones. She was better now. During the storm she had squatted with hunched shoulders on the carpet like a native in his hut, letting the waves of sound and light break over her. It was generally thought she had some coloured blood. But this, now that she had begun to reveal such visible proof of her glamorous fortune and character, was no bar to the society of the vet, the chemist and the clergyman. Many of the doctors from the clinic visited her and were enchanted by her eccentric grandeur, and much preferred her company to that of the tropical-skinned vet's wife and the watery-blonde chemist's wife and the music-loving clergyman's wife, at sultry sundowner times in the rainy season. My brother Richard was fascinated by Sonia.

We nurses were astonished that the men were so dazzled. She was our creature, our folly, our lark. We had lavished our imagination upon her eager mind and had ourselves designed the long voile 'afternoon' dresses, and had ourselves put it to her that she must have a path leading down to the river and a punt on the little river and a pink parasol to go with the punt. There was something in the air of the place that affected the men, even those newly out from England, with an overturn of discrimination. One of the research workers at the clinic had already married a brassy barmaid from Johannesburg, another had married a neurotic dressmaker from the Cape who seemed to have dozens of elbows, so much did she throw her long bony arms about. We too were subject to the influence of the place but we did not think of this when we were engrossed in our bizarre cultivation of Sonia and our dressing her up to kill. At the time, we only saw the men taking our fantasy in earnest, and looked at each other, smiled and looked away.

In the year before Jannie Van der Merwe was due to be released from prison I spent much of my free time at Sonia's with my brother Richard. Her house was by now a general meeting-place for the district and she conducted quite a salon every late afternoon. About this time I became engaged to marry a research worker at the clinic.

I do not know if Richard slept with Sonia. He was very

enamoured of her and would not let anyone make fun of her in his hearing.

She said one day: 'Why d'you want to marry that Frank? Man, he looks like your brother, you want to catch a fellow that doesn't look like one of the family. I could get you a fellow more your type.'

I was irritated by this. I kept Frank from seeing her as much as possible; but it was not possible; all our lives outside the clinic seemed to revolve round Sonia. When Frank began to ridicule Sonia I knew he was in some way, which he was afraid to admit, attracted by her.

She chattered incessantly, her voice accented in the Afrikaans way. I had to admire her quick grasp of every situation, for now she was acquainted with the inner politics of the clinic, and managed to put in effective words here and there with visiting Government officials who took it for granted she had ruled the district for years and, being above the common run, pleased herself how she dressed and what she did.

I heard her discussing our disagreeable chief radiologist with an important member of the Medical Board: 'Man, he got high spirits I tell you, man. I see him dig the spurs into the horse when he pass my house every morning, he goes riding to work off those high spirits. But I tell one thing, he's good at his job. Man, he's first rate at the job.' Soon after this our ill-tempered radiologist, who did not ride very frequently, was transferred to another district. It was only when I heard that the important man from the Medical Board was a fanatical horse-lover that I realized the full force of Sonia's abilities.

'God, what have we done?' I said to my best friend.

She said, 'Leave well alone. She's getting us a new wing.'

Sonia made plans to obtain for Richard the job of Chief

Medical Officer in the north. I suspected that Sonia meant to follow him to the north if he should be established there, for she had remarked one day that she would have to get used to travel; it must be easy: 'Man, everyone does it. Drink up. Cheerio.'

Frank had also applied for the job. He said – looking at the distance with his short-sighted eyes, which gave to his utterances a suggestion of disinterestedness – 'I've got better qualifications for it than Richard.' So he had. 'Richard is the better research worker,' Frank said. This was true. 'Richard should stay here and I should go up north,' Frank said. 'You would like it up there,' he said. All this was undeniable.

It became apparent very soon that Frank was competing with Richard for Sonia's attention. He did this without appearing to notice it himself, as if it were some routine performance in the clinic, not the method but the results of which interested him. I could hardly believe the ridiculous carry-on of these two men.

'Do they think she will really have any influence in the question of that job?'

'Yes,' my best friend said, 'and so she will.'

That important member of the Medical Board – he who was passionate about horses – was in the district again. He had come for a long week-end's fishing. It was all mad. There was no big fishing at Fort Beit.

I began to want Richard to get the job. I cooled off where Frank was concerned; he did not notice, but I cooled off. Richard had become highly nervous. As soon as he had free time he raced off in his car to Sonia's. Frank, who was less scrupulous about taking free time, was usually there first.

I was at the tea-party when the ageing, loose-mouthed, keen-eyed chief of the Medical Board turned up. Richard and Frank sat at opposite ends of a sofa. Richard looked embarrassed; I knew he was thinking of the job, and trying not to seem to be exploiting his attachment to Sonia. I sat near them. Sonia, reciting a long formula from her book of etiquette, introduced us to the important man. As she did so it struck me that this recitation might to some ears sound like a charming gesture against the encroaching slackness of the times. She sat the man between Richard and Frank, and clearly she meant business.

She stood by. She had a beautiful shape; we nurses had not provided that, we had only called it forth from the peasant slouch. She said to the old man, 'Richard yere wants to talk to you, Basil, man,' and touched Richard's shoulder. Frank was peering into the abstract distance. It occurred to me that Frank was the administrative type; none of the research workers I had known were dispassionate, they were vulnerable and nervous.

Richard was nervous. He did not look at the man, he was looking up at Sonia's face with its West-End make-up.

'Applied for the job up north?' said this Basil to Richard.

'Yes,' Richard said, and smiled with relief.

'Want it?' said the man, casually, in his great importance.

'Oh, rather,' Richard said.

'Well, have it,' said the man, flicking away the invisible job with his forefinger as lightly as if it were a ping-pong ball.

'Well,' Richard said, 'no thank you.'

'What did you say?' said the man.

'What that you say?' said Sonia.

My brother and I are very unlike in most ways, but there are a few radical points of similarity between us. It must be something in the blood.

'No thank you,' Richard was saying. 'After all, I feel I ought to go on with research in tropical diseases.'

Sonia's fury only made a passing pattern on her face. Her

first thought was for the old man, fussed and suddenly groundless as he was. 'Basil, man,' she said, bending over him with her breasts about his ears, 'you got the wrong chap. This yere Frank is the boy I was talking of to you. Frank, may I have the honour to introduce to you this yere distinguished – '

'Yes, we've met,' said the man, turning to Frank.

Frank returned from the middle distance. 'I've applied for the job,' he said, 'and my qualifications are, I think – '

'Married?'

'No, but hoping to be.' He turned duly to me and I smiled back most nastily.

'Want the job?'

'Oh, rather.'

'Sure?'

'Oh yes, quite sure.'

The old man was not going to be caught again. 'I hope you really want the job. There are a good many excellent applicants and we want a keen – '

'Yes, I want the job.'

Sonia said, 'Well, have it,' and I thought, then, she had really done for the whole thing and outrun her influence.

But the old man beamed up at her, took both her prettily-restored hands in his, and I nearly saw his slack mouth water.

Other people were pressing round for a word with this Medical Board man. Sonia was treating Richard with ostentatious neglect. Frank was leaning against the wall, now, talking to her. Suddenly I did not want to lose Frank. I looked round the company and wondered what I was doing there, and said to Richard, 'Let's go.'

Richard was looking at Sonia's back. 'Why do you want to go?' Richard said. 'It's early yet. Why?'

Because the curtain was fluttering at the open window,

letting in wafts of the savage territory beyond the absurd drawing-room. The people were getting excited; I thought soon they might scream, once or twice like the birds, and then be silent. I thought, even, that Richard might change his mind again about the job, and tell Sonia so, and leave it to her to sort it out for him. It was the pull of Sonia that made him reluctant to leave. She was adjusting Frank's tie and telling him he needed looking after, for all the world as if she had been brought up to that old line; we must tell her, I thought, not to do that sort of thing in public. And I would gladly have stayed on till sundowner time in order to jerk Frank back into a sense of my personality; but there was a storm coming, and it was no fun driving home through a storm.

Richard is stronger-willed than I am. After this party he kept away from Sonia's and stuck in to his work. I broke off my engagement. It was impossible to know whether Frank was relieved or not. There were still three months before he was to take up his appointment in the north. He spent most of his time with Sonia. I was not sure how things stood between them. I still drove over to Sonia's sometimes and found Frank there. I was dissatisfied and attracted by both of them and by their situation. In the dry spells they would often be down the river in the punt when I arrived, and I would wait for the sight of the returning pink parasol, and be glad of the sight. Once or twice when we met at the clinic Frank said to me, factually, 'We could still be married.' Once he said, 'Old Sonia's only a joke, you know.' But I thought he was afraid I might take him at his word, or might do so too soon.

Sonia spoke again of travelling. She was learning to study road maps. She told one of the nurses, 'When Frank's settled up at the north I'll go up and settle him down nicer.' She told another of the nurses, 'My old husband's coming

64

from gaol this month, next month, I don't know, man. He'll see some changes. He get used to them.'

One afternoon I drove over to the farm; I had not seen Sonia for six weeks because her children had been home for the holidays and I loathed her children. I had missed her, she was never boring. The house-boy said she was down the river with Dr Frank. I wandered down the path, but they were not in sight. I waited for about eight minutes and walked back. All the natives except the house-boy had gone to sleep in their huts. I did not see the house-boy for some time, and when I did I was frightened by the fear on his face.

I was coming round by the old ox-stalls, now deserted – since Sonia had abandoned farming, even with a tractor, far less a span of oxen. The house-boy appeared then, and whispered to me. 'Baas Van der Merwe is come. He looking in the window.'

I walked quietly round the stalls till I had a view of the house, and saw a man of about fifty, undernourished-looking, in khaki shorts and shirt. He was standing on a box by the drawing-room window. He had his hand on the curtain, parting it, and was looking steadily into the empty room.

'Go down to the river and warn them,' I said to the boy.

He turned to go, but 'Boy!' shouted the man. The house-boy in his green-and-white clothes rapidly went towards the voice.

I got down to the river just as they were landing. Sonia was dressed in pale blue. Her new parasol was blue. She looked specially fabulous and I noticed her very white teeth, her round brown eyes and her story-book pose, as she stood dressed up in the middle of Africa under the blazing sun with the thick-leaved plants at her feet. Frank, looking nice in tropical suiting, was tying up the punt. 'Your husband has returned,' I said, and ran fearfully back to my car. I started it up and made off, and as I sped past the house over the gravel I saw Jannie Van der Merwe about to enter the house, followed by the servant. He turned to watch my car and spoke to the native, evidently asking who I was.

Afterwards the native deposed that Jannie went all through the house examining the changes and the new furniture. He used the lavatory and pulled the chain. He tried the taps in both bathrooms. In Sonia's room he put straight a pair of her shoes which were lying askew. He then tested all the furniture for dust, all through the house, touching the furniture with the middle finger of his right hand and turning up his finger to see if it showed any dust. The house-boy followed, and when Jannie came to an old oak Dutch chest which was set away in a corner of one of the children's rooms – since Sonia had taken against all her father's old furniture – he found a little dust on it. He ordered the native to fetch a duster and remove the dust. When this was done Jannie proceeded on his tour, and when he had tried everything for dust he went out and down the path towards the river. He found Sonia and Frank at the ox-stalls arguing about what to do and where to go, and taking a revolver from his pocket, shot them. Sonia died immediately. Frank lingered for ten hours. This was a serious crime and Jannie was hanged.

I waited all the weeks ahead for Richard to make the first suggestion that we should move away. I was afraid to suggest it first lest he should resent the move all his life. Our long leave was not due for another year. Our annual leave was not due for some months. At last he said, 'I can't stand it here.'

I wanted to return to England. I had been thinking of nothing else.

'We can't stay here,' I said, as if it were a part in a play.

'Shall we pack up and go?' he said, and I felt a huge relief.

'No,' I said.

He said, 'It would be a pity to pack it all in when we've both gone so far in tropical diseases.'

In fact I left the following week. Since then, Richard has gone far in tropical diseases. 'It's a pity,' he said before I left, 'to let what's happened come between us.'

I packed up my things and departed for dear life, before the dry season should set in, and the rainy season should follow, and all things be predictable.

The Playhouse Called Remarkable

I was telling my friend Moon Biglow the other day that I was going to Hampstead to see some literary people.

'Oh, littery people,' said Moon – because that's how he talks.

'Oh, Hampstead!' said Moon.

'Yes,' I said. 'I'm going to read a story to illustrate the Uprise of my Downfall.'

Moon turned a little jerky. It's strange how you think you know people, and then they do something odd, and you have to start on virgin ground again.

'What's the matter, Moon?' I asked him. We were sitting in a milk-bar drinking coffee, or whatever it really was.

'Have another coffee,' I suggested.

'*The Uprise*,' said Moon, '*of your Downfall*? Did you say . . .'

'Oh,' I said hastily, 'it's got nothing to do with the Fall of Man, you know. This is just a way of expressing my venture into that bourne from which no traveller returns, I mean . . .'

'Then you know the secret!' Moon exclaimed.

'Secret?' I said. 'There's no secret about it. It comes to me naturally.

'A mere gift,' I added modestly.

I was thinking of some means of extracting myself from Moon's company. I didn't like the look of him in the least, desperately afraid of me for some reason.

Suddenly Moon's will seemed to slump. I said I must go.

'Don't go until you've told me how you came to *know*.' Moon was quite mild now, quite blank.

'Know *what*?' I said impatiently. 'What *have* you been drinking?'

'Either tea or coffee,' Moon replied, gazing into his cup, for he was extremely truthful. One thing about Moon, he is always very fond of the truth.

'The uprise of your downfall,' said Moon. 'I must say when you came out with it just now, I was fit to bust, but I'll get over it in a day or two. Only tell me how . . .'

'That phrase,' I said, 'refers to my downward progress up to the dizzy heights, as they concern the art of letters.'

'I *know*,' said Moon, 'I mean,' he added, having conceived a new thought, 'I *think* I know.'

I said, 'What are you talking about and why are you talking in italics?'

'*You* say first,' said Moon suspiciously, 'what *you're* talking about.'

'Nothing doing,' I said mysteriously – because I'd begun to get interested in the thing in Moon's mind.

'Well,' said Moon, 'it's the Moon, isn't it?'

'Yes,' I said, because I never have scruples about artistic lies.

Moon breathed a long draught of invisible nourishment from the air, then sighed it out again.

'Anything else?' Moon enquired.

'Hampstead,' I ventured, remembering that this word had started him off.

'Ah,' said Moon. 'Well, now, I'll tell you the *true* story, because whoever told you the secret has ten to one told you the wrong thing. You'll get the truth from me.'

Before I tell you Moon Biglow's story, I must tell you something about him. He's the sort of friend whose family and background you know nothing about. I always felt he came from Ireland or Chicago or somewhere like that – because of the name, rather strange, of Moon Biglow. Moon must be about forty, and he describes himself as a freelance, which I suppose means journalism once a month. The strange thing is, I can't remember where I first met Moon. It was probably at a party. I must have known him for ten years. I would often see him in Kensington High Street in the late morning, short and fair and dressed in brown. His face is small, but his features are big, a pleasant face. I doubt if I shall see it again for some time, for Moon has left London now.

Well, to get back to the story that Moon Biglow told me when I was downcast about my downfall rising up.

'I used to live at Hampstead,' said Moon. 'That was just after the Flood.'

'Did they have a flood?' I said. 'When would that be?'

'The *Flood*,' said Moon. 'I mean Noah's Flood – the big one. You just listen to me. I'm telling no lies.'

'I lived at Hampstead just after the Flood. Of course, it was very different then, but there was a pleasant little society of people – long before the palaeolithic savages appeared, of course. The son of Noah called Ham begat this particular crowd – hence the name Hampstead. There were six of us,' said Moon, 'six to begin with – later seven. Of course, we were total strangers to the place, but everyone made us welcome.'

'Where had you come from?' I asked.

'The Moon,' said Moon. 'You know that very well. Don't interrupt me with insincere questions. We came of our own free will on the Downfall of our Uprise, and we settled at Hampstead; seeing it was the most civilized place on the globe in the post-Flood years. It was almost like the Moon – of course, the Moon has changed since then, but I remember the Moon in her prime. She was a beauty to live on. Still, we left her and came to settle in Hampstead.

'The nice thing about the people,' said Moon, 'was their discretion. They never enquired why we came, they simply accepted us.'

'After the first eighteen months, when the ice was broken, we told them why we had come to earth. We got the Mayor of Hampstead and his wife to call a meeting at the Town Hall. That was where Keats's house is now. I wrote out my speech and learnt it by heart. Of course, I was more eloquent in those days than I am now. I still remember every word.

'"Friends, brothers and sisters," I said, "The Six Brothers of the Moon give you greeting, and beg the privilege, nay the honour, of addressing your inmost hearts. There will, brothers and sisters, sisters and brothers, – there will come a time when these words will no longer reverberate new and thrilling to the ear. And why? Will your progeny, generation upon generation, remained unmoved by a brotherly sppeal to the heart of man? No. Why then, will they shun and mock at such a speech as I deliver to you this evening? – For upon my prophetic honour, they will do so. They will call it, my friends, empty rhetoric. They will term it by the names of blah, drip, ham, and bloody awful.

'"That things should not be otherwise than thus, my brothers and my sisters, is in the nature of this earth, your home. I need not dwell on the cycles of birth, growth, decay and death, which you sum up in your profound philosophy, 'Nothing lasts long.' It is the same, my dear children, with all expressions of life, and if I may say so without offence to that tenderness, that ineffable refinement of spirit which I perceive within you, your language is in a shocking condition. As for your art, it does not exist.

'"Sisters, we are come from the Moon to teach you the language of poetry. Brothers, we are here on what you might term an art mission."'

At this point Moon Biglow stopped talking and took a large bite from a Chelsea bun. As you can imagine, I was somewhat puzzled by his story. If you had met Moon

Biglow, you would never doubt the sincerity of the man. There was something very honest, also, about the way he was eating the bun; it seemed as undebatable as the story he was telling. Of course, I wanted to question him, but decided this might put him off. As a provisional measure, I worked it out that either he was mad or that he was not mad.

'What happened next?' I said.

'Well,' said Moon, 'I finished my speech, shook hands with the gentlemen, kissed all the ladies, and went home to bed.'

I could see that somehow I had hurt Moon's feelings.

'*Do* tell me what transpired,' I said urgently.

'I am *not* mad,' said Moon; then he continued his story.

'To tell you the truth,' said Moon, 'the whole race of Hampstead was dying out from the sheer lack of something to do in its spare time. They had only one recreation. In the evenings they would get together at the local Welfare Centre. All they did was to sit on the floor and chant. The chant went like this: Tum tum *ya*, tum tum *ya* – the same thing over and over again. Nothing else. Just tum tum *ya* the whole evening until they were tired. And it was the same every night. Naturally, at this rate, the race was beginning to die out.

'Well, we put it to them that what we had to offer was a very good thing. We proposed to set up a playhouse at Hampstead, and give nightly performances for a small fee. We proposed to bring them the Changing Drama of the Moon. I told them,' said Moon. '"Once you have seen and heard the Changing Drama of the Moon," I said, "you will never more be content, my friends, with your own national classic, the Unchanging Tum tum *ya*. It is not," I added, "that we of the Moon do not hold the classical tradition in the greatest possible reverence. But you will have observed amongst yourselves that the time-honoured tum tum *ya* no longer possesses the power to keep you interested in life. Many of your youth have died from the disease of boredom. No babies have been born for the past two years.

'"Friends," I concluded, "the tum tum *ya* is not enough."

'We had only one opponent – young Johnnie Heath, assistant editor of the *Tum Tum Times*. Johnnie set up the slogan: "Hampstead for the sons of Ham," and pasted up bills all over the town with headlines like "Down With the Moon," and "Protect our Women from the Arty Crafties." But no one took any notice of Johnnie Heath – there was terrific excitement over the new scheme. We took over the Welfare Centre and got it reconstructed into a large theatre. First we called it the Moon Playhouse, but Johnnie Heath started agitating about this name, so to keep him quiet we changed it simply to the Playhouse.

'The opening night was a tremendous triumph. I must tell you something about the Changing Drama of the Moon.

'The artists of the Moon had only one principal theme, and this was the story on which our show was based. It happens to be a true story. On top of a high mountain on the Moon there was at that time a singing voice. It did not sing in words, only pure notes. There had always been much speculation on the Moon as to whether this was a man's voice or a woman's voice; it was very difficult to tell. From time to time an expedition sets out to the singing mountain to try to locate the singer. The approach to the singing mountain was pitted with deep concealed craters. No one had ever returned from an expedition. But there was once a young girl, an acrobat and singer by profession, who taught herself to mimic the voice. She decided to fit its music to words, and set off for the mountain, intending to find out what inspired the singer. If she knew the source of the melody, she would know what words to fit in.

'By her acrobatic skill, this Moon girl managed to reach

73

the mountain, swinging from rock to tree to rock. All the people in that territory of the Moon could hear her singing to cheer herself up as she climbed the mountain, because it was night. She sang a song about her journey, the warm, strange-smelling forests and the lakes of phosphorus. As she approached the top, the song combined with the voice of the singing mountain like a duet. She reached the summit at dawn. Suddenly the Moon girl was silent. Only the mountain notes could be heard. The people waited anxiously all that day for some sign from the Moon girl, but no sound came. Towards evening they gave her up as lost. She had been murdered, they concluded, by the jealous voice of the mountain.

'But just as the sun had set, they heard a cry from the mountain-top. The Moon girl began to sing again, her voice beating against the mountain melody in a kind of desperate dialogue. It made a strange harmony. The Moon girl sang a narrative song which told how she was imprisoned by the voice of the mountain. The voice, she sang, had no body attached to it, but it surrounded her and held her fast on the mountain peak in a whirling spiral of sound. She could not move to left or right, neither forward nor backward, but was compelled to spin round and round with the voice of the mountain spirit. Our Moon girl is still there. She pirouettes on the mountain peak every night, imprisoned in the spinning voice, and singing a continual song of defiance, in harmony with her prisoner, the mountain spirit. Every day at sunrise she stops singing, and her whirling body comes to a standstill. On clear days the Moon people can make out her small figure standing motionless on the mountain peak while the voice of the mountain mocks her with its high wordless music. Eventually the Moon girl told us in her song how it is that she can't make any sound or movement during the day. Every morning there is a certain ray of the sun which stabs her through the throat more sharply than a fine steel blade. She is pinioned against the sky throughout the day, unable to cry or move until the terrible blade of the sun withdraws itself from her throat at nightfall. The Moon girl's song tells us that this hard ray of the sun is what inspires the musical mountain. And the Moon girl sings of other things too. She tells us in her nightly song all she has seen on the landscape of the moon. It was the Moon girl who told us in her song to bring her drama to the earth.'

Moon Biglow was beginning to look dreary. He was obviously much taken up with this Moon girl, and seemed likely to discourse upon the wonder of the lady all morning.

'What about your Playhouse?' I said, ' – at Hampstead, you know.'

'Yes,' said Moon. 'I was just coming down to earth.'

'Well,' he continued, 'we put on the Changing Drama of the Moon, based on this history of the Moon girl – that's the active part of it, the drama. The Changing part comes in the words and music; because, you see, the Moon girl sings a different song every night. She saves up everything she sees by day, and hurls it in her song against the walls of the voice which imprisons her.

'And so we followed her story; we showed her journey to the mountain – dancing and singing. We reproduced her changing dialogue with the mountain, reproaching the invisible voice with everything under the sun – we put the glittering blue salt-banks on the shores of the Moon lakes into human language; we satirized the incoming tides of the earth, and the landmarks of Hampstead Heath from season to season; we even put our enemy Johnnie Heath to music, to try and placate him, praising his intelligence. But he didn't care for it much. Our decor was magnificent. Since we took it from the shapes and colours of the Moon, no one had seen anything like it.

'No one, in fact, had seen anything like our Playhouse show before. It was a tremendous success. We had to extend the premises, for the Playhouse had become a sort of communal centre.

'"A remarkable performance," everyone said. "Quite remarkable."

'In fact the Playhouse came to be known as the Remarkable. People would arrange to meet each other at the Remarkable, and we six Moon Brothers were known as the Young Remarkables. A new spirit had entered the people of Hampstead. Not only were they wildly in love with the Moon girl whose history and whose changing song we depicted nightly, but they were more in love with each other. The youth of the community stopped dying young; the maternity wards opened again; the Remarkable was packed to the doors each evening.

'For my part, I was in love with Dolores, the daughter of the Mayor of Hampstead. We had not brought any girls from the moon, as the earth doesn't agree with the Moonish female. So we got Dolores to play the part of the Moon girl, which she did in a most lifelike manner. Of course, we were all six fond of Dolores, but eventually she became attached to me.

'This was about five years after we opened the Remarkable. Then Dolores' father, the Mayor, died, and we were all very irritated when Johnnie Heath took his place. The *Tum Tum Times* was, of course, no longer functioning, but Johnnie had worked himself up on some of the new civic welfare plans occasioned by the revitalized life of the community. He was becoming very influential.

'We had planned to branch off into a new field and set up a sort of academy of art. Perhaps it was just as well we never got the chance, but our reasons were quite *reasonable*. Although the Remarkable show continued to flourish, we somehow couldn't induce the people to practise any form of our art themselves. No Hampstead poets, no painters, no musicians. The general feeling was that art was a Moon affair; and only the Young Remarkables could really handle it. When we pointed out how well Dolores expressed the Moon girl, they replied that she was a bit of a born Moon girl herself. Perhaps they were right. We never got very far with our academic project, and some months after Johnnie Heath became the Mayor, we began to have difficulties with the Playhouse called Remarkable. Johnnie had somehow introduced an acid note into the life of Hampstead. (It was a descendant of Johnnie's, by the way, who founded the London School of Economics.)

'He started a campaign of enquiry against us. We had to fill in forms about our origin. We had to fill in an enormous questionnaire for our licence to run the Playhouse.

'On the grounds that we were not born on earth, and because there was no evidence of life on the Moon, Johnnie tried to prove that we did not exist at all. He sent us an official note objecting to our description of the Playhouse. He could not accept the phrase "known as the Remarkable", he wrote, and begged to point out that whereas "Playhouse" was a noun, "Remarkable" was an adjective. The two could not be reconciled as signifying one and the same object.

'As the year wore on, so did Johnnie's nuisance-campaign. His tone became more and more peremptory. He tightened up on the vigilance of the police, and we were frequently fined for small infringements.

'Johnnie defeated us, in fact. We gave our last performance one evening in February. It was seven years since our first performance. The people were very upset, but Johnnie had so worked on them that they were afraid to express their grief.

'We had decided to take Dolores back to the Moon with us, in the usual way, you know.'

'What way?' I asked, eagerly.

'Don't interrupt,' said Moon. 'And anyhow you know the

way to the Moon. You go on the Uprise of your Downfall, you told me yourself!'

'Listen,' I said desperately, 'I know nothing about how to get to the Moon. There's a lot of talk about space-ships, but what have they got to do with the Uprise . . .?'

'Quite,' said Moon. 'Quite.'

I had better say straight away that so far as getting to the Moon is concerned, that was all the information I extracted from Moon Biglow. It has something to do with uprising and downfalling, we may be sure. But the end of his story is still to be told.

'On what I thought was my last night on earth,' Moon continued, 'I took a walk over Hampstead Heath. We had closed the doors of the Remarkable for the last time and were all prepared for the last Uprise of our Downfall. Dolores was to come with us. We were both sorry and glad to go. We felt sad about leaving Hampstead, but the place and people had changed under Johnnie's influence, and also largely under our own in the last seven years.

'I brooded on these things and was turning back to our quarters where I was to meet Dolores, when suddenly I heard a curious sound on my right.

'As I walked towards the place, I became aware that a number of people were gathered together hidden from my sight behind a large boulder. Presently I could hear more clearly what the noise was: these people were chanting together the old refrain. Tum tum *ya*, tum tum *ya*. Silently, I peered round the boulder, and stopped short, sick and terrified and appalled by what I saw.

'Before I describe what I saw, I must tell you that Johnnie Heath had recently revived the *Tum Tum Times*. One of its columns was regularly devoted to a plea for a return to what was described variously as "the native purity of our customs", or "the purity of our native customs", or else "the customs of our native purity". I had not thought very much about this, for Johnnie's ideas were always rather cranky. But one day I had chanced to read in this column a reference to an organization which was recommended as offering "an outlet through a classical mode of expressions of our most pure and primitive passions". On reading this, I shuddered, then thought no more about it.

'I remembered this some time after the incident on Hampstead Heath.

'Now,' said Moon Biglow, 'I will tell you what I saw there.

'A group of young men and women, well known to me, and many of whom had been close friends, were seated cross-legged in a circle round a stone slab. By the light of the Moon I saw them led by Johnnie Heath clapping their hands to the rhythm of tum tum *ya*, tum tum *ya*. On the slab inside the circle lay the dead body of Dolores, with a knife stuck in her throat. The blood was congealed on her neck, where it had flowed and ceased to flow.

'Then I saw, watching from behind them, two of my Moon Brothers. They moved round silently to where I was standing. Hand in hand we fled home.

'My five Moon Brothers left the earth secretly during the night. I could not, myself, face the Moon without Dolores. I felt it necessary to remain on earth and die here where she died.

'Of course, I cleared out of Hampstead.

'But the strange thing is, that our mission wasn't a failure, after all. The revival of the tum tum *ya* cult did not last. It still crops up from time to time here and there, for these things spread. But the absence of the Changing Drama of the Moon began to be felt. The sense of loss led to a tremendous movement of the human spirit. The race of the artist appeared on the earth, everywhere attempting to express the lost Moon drama. Long after the people who had frequented the old Remarkable Playhouse were dead and forgotten the legend survived; and long after the legend was forgotten, the sense of loss survived.

'So it happens,' said Moon Biglow, 'that whenever the tum tum *ya* movement gets afoot, and the monotony and horror start taking hold of people, the artists rise up and proclaim the virtue of the remarkable things that are missing from the earth.

'And so,' said Moon Biglow, 'you owe your literature, your symphonies, your old masters and your new masters, to the Six Moon Brothers and Dolores. It was a good thing we had to go. We could never have induced you to shift for yourselves by any other means.'

'You and your littery friends,' said Moon Biglow, 'ought to know the true position, which is what I've told you. And if ever you produce a decent poem or a story, it won't be on account of anything you've got in this world but of something remarkable which you haven't got. There is always a call for the Remarkable from time to time, simply because we closed the doors of the Playhouse called Remarkable, and because the Young Remarkables have gone off home, and because there is nothing left Remarkable beneath the visiting Moon.'

The Ormolu Clock

The Hotel Stroh stood side by side with the Guesthouse Lublonitsch, separated by a narrow path that led up the mountain, on the Austrian side, to the Yugoslavian border. Perhaps the old place had once been a great hunting tavern. These days, though, the Hotel Stroh was plainly a disappointment to its few drooping tenants. They huddled together like birds in a storm; their flesh sagged over the unscrubbed tables on the dark back veranda, which looked over Herr Stroh's untended fields. Usually, Herr Stroh sat somewhat apart, in a mist of cognac, his lower chin resting on his red neck, and his shirt open for air. Those visitors who had come not for the climbing but simply for the view sat and admired the mountain and were sloppily waited upon until the weekly bus should come and carry them away. If they had cars, they rarely stayed long – they departed, as a rule, within two hours of arrival, like a comic act. This much was entertainingly visible from the other side of the path, at the Guesthouse Lublonitsch.

I was waiting for friends to come and pick me up on their way to Venice. Frau Lublonitsch welcomed all her guests in person. When I arrived I was hardly aware of the honour, she seemed so merely a local woman – undefined and dumpy – as she emerged from the kitchen wiping her hands on her brown apron, with her grey hair drawn back tight, her sleeves rolled up, her dingy dress, black stockings, and boots. It was only gradually that her importance was permitted to dawn upon strangers.

There was a Herr Lublonitsch, but he was of no account, even though he got all the marital courtesies. He sat punily with his drinking friends at one of the tables in front of the inn, greeting the guests as they passed in and out and receiving as much attention as he wanted from the waitresses. When he was sick Frau Lublonitsch took his meals with her own hands to a room upstairs set aside for his sickness. But she was undoubtedly the boss.

She worked the hired girls fourteen hours a day, and they did the work cheerfully. She was never heard to complain or to give an order; it was enough that she was there. Once, when a girl dropped a tray with five mugs of soup, Frau Lublonitsch went and fetched a cloth and submissively mopped up the mess herself, like any old peasant who had suffered worse than that in her time. The maids called her Frau Chef. 'Frau Chef prepares special food when her husband's stomach is bad,' one of them told me.

Appended to the guesthouse was a butcher's shop, and this was also a Lublonitsch possession. A grocer's shop had been placed beside it, and on an adjacent plot of ground – all Lublonitsch property – a draper's shop was nearing completion. Two of her sons worked in the butcher's establishment; a third had been placed in charge of the grocer's; and the youngest son, now ready to take his place, was destined for the draper's.

In the garden, strangely standing on a path between the flowers for decorating the guests' tables and the vegetables for eating, facing the prolific orchard and overhung by the chestnut trees that provided a roof for outdoor diners, grew one useless thing – a small, well-tended palm tree. It gave an air to the place. Small as it was, this alien plant stood as high as the distant mountain peaks when seen from the perspective of the great back porch where we dined. It quietly dominated the view.

Ordinarily, I got up at seven, but one morning I woke at half-past five and came down from my room on the second floor to the yard, to find someone to make me some coffee. Standing in the sunlight, with her back to me, was Frau Lublonitsch. She was regarding her wide kitchen garden, her fields beyond it, her outbuildings and her pigsties where two aged women were already at work. One of the sons emerged from an outbuilding carrying several strings of long sausages. Another led a bullock with a bag tied over its head to a tree and chained it there to await the slaughterers. Frau Lublonitsch did not move but continued to survey her property, her pigs, her pig-women, her chestnut trees, her beanstalks, her sausages, her sons, her tall gladioli, and – as if she had eyes in the back of her head – she seemed aware, too, of the good thriving guesthouse behind her, and the butcher's shop, the draper's shop, and the grocer's.

Just as she turned to attack the day's work, I saw that she glanced at the sorry Hotel Stroh across the path. I saw her mouth turn down at the corners with the amusement of one who has a certain foreknowledge; I saw a landowner's recognition in her little black eyes.

You could tell, even before the local people told you, that Frau Lublonitsch had built up the whole thing from nothing by her own wits and industry. But she worked pitiably hard. She did all the cooking. She supervised the household, and, without moving hurriedly, she sped into the running of the establishment like the maniac drivers from Vienna who tore along the highroad in front of her place. She scoured the huge pans herself, wielding her podgy arm round and round; clearly, she trusted none of the girls to do the job properly. She was not above sweeping the floor, feeding the pigs, and serving in the butcher's shop, where she would patiently hold one after another great sausage under her customer's nose for him to smell its quality. She did not sit down, except to take her dinner in the kitchen, from her rising at dawn to her retiring at one in the morning.

83

Why does she do it, what for? Her sons are grown up, she's got her guesthouse, her servants, her shops, her pigs, fields, cattle –

At the café across the river, where I went in the late afternoon, they said, 'Frau Lublonitsch has got far more than that. She owns all the strip of land up to the mountain. She's got three farms. She may even expand across the river and down this way to the town.'

'Why does she work so hard? She dresses like a peasant,' they said. 'She scours the pots.' Frau Lublonitsch was their favourite subject.

She did not go to church, she was above church. I had hoped to see her there, wearing different clothes and perhaps sitting with the chemist, the dentist, and their wives in the second front row behind the count and his family; or perhaps she might have taken some less notice-able place among the congregation. But Frau Lublonitsch was a church unto herself, and even resembled in shape the onion-shaped spires of the churches around her.

I climbed the lower slopes of the mountains while the experts in their boots did the thing earnestly up on the sheer crags about the clouds. When it rained, they came back and reported, 'Tito is sending the bad weather.' The maids were bored with the joke, but they obliged with smiles every time, and served them up along with the interminable veal.

The higher mountain reaches were beyond me except by bus. I was anxious, however, to scale the peaks of Frau Lublonitsch's nature.

One morning, when everything was glittering madly after a nervous stormy night, I came down early to look for coffee. I had heard voices in the yard some moments before, but by the time I appeared they had gone indoors. I followed the voices to the dark stone kitchen and peered in the doorway. Beyond the chattering girls, I caught sight of a further doorway, which usually remained closed. Now it was open.

Within it was a bedroom reaching far back into the house. It was imperially magnificent. It was done in red and gold. I saw a canopied bed, built high, splendidly covered with a scarlet quilt. The pillows were piled up at the head – about four of them, very white. The bed-head was deep dark wood, touched with gilt. A golden fringe hung from the canopy. In some ways this bed reminded me of the glowing bed by which van Eyck ennobled the portrait of Jan Arnolfini and his wife. All the rest of the Lublonitsch establishment was scrubbed and polished local wood, but this was a very poetic bed.

The floor of the bedroom was covered with a carpet of red which was probably crimson but which, against the scarlet of the bed, looked purple. On the walls on either side of the bed hung Turkish carpets whose background was an opulently dull, more ancient red – almost black where the canopy cast its shade.

I was moved by the sight. The girl called Mitzi was watching me as I stood in the kitchen doorway. 'Coffee?' she said.

'Whose room is that?'

'It's Frau Chef's room. She sleeps there.'

Now another girl, tall, lanky Gertha, with her humorous face and slightly comic answer to everything, skipped over to the bedroom door and said, 'We are instructed to keep the door closed,' and for a moment before closing it she drew open the door quite wide for me to see some more of the room. I caught sight of a tiled stove constructed of mosaic tiles that were not a local type; they were lustrous – ochre and green – resembling the tiles on the floors of Byzantine ruins. The stove looked like a temple. I saw a black lacquered cabinet inlaid with mother-of-pearl, and just before Gertha closed the door I noticed, standing upon the cabinet, a large ornamental clock, its case enamelled rosily with miniature inset pastel paintings; each curve and twirl in the case of this clock was overlaid with that gilded-bronze alloy which is known as ormolu. The clock twinkled in the early sunlight which slanted between the window hangings.

I went into the polished dining-room, and Mitzi brought my coffee there. From the window I could see Frau Lublonitsch in her dark dress, her black boots and wool stockings. She was plucking a chicken over a bucketful of feathers. Beyond her I could see the sulky figure of Herr Stroh standing collarless, fat and unshaven, in the open door of his hotel across the path. He seemed to be meditating upon Frau Lublonitsch.

It was that very day that the nuisance occurred. The double windows of my bedroom were directly opposite the bedroom windows of the Hotel Stroh, with no more than twenty feet between – the width of the narrow path that led up to the frontier.

It was a cold day. I sat in my room writing letters. I glanced out of the window. In the window directly opposite me stood Herr Stroh, gazing blatantly upon me. I was annoyed at his interest. I pulled down the blind and switched on the light to continue my writing. I wondered if Herr Stroh had seen me doing anything peculiar before I had noticed him, such as tapping my head with the end of my pen or scratching my nose or pulling at my chin, or one of the things one might do while writing a letter. The drawn blind and the artificial light irritated me, and suddenly I didn't see why I shouldn't write my letters by daylight without being stared at. I switched off the light and released the blind. Herr Stroh had gone. I concluded that he had taken my action as a signal of disapproval, and I settled back to write.

I looked up a few moments later, and this time Herr

Stroh was seated on a chair a little way back from the window. He was facing me squarely and holding to his eyes a pair of field-glasses.

I left my room and went down to complain to Frau Lublonitsch.

.'She's gone to market,' Gertha said. 'She'll be back in half an hour.'

So I lodged my complaint with Gertha.

'I shall tell Frau Chef,' she said.

Something in her manner made me ask, 'Has this ever happened before?'

'Once or twice this year,' she said. 'I'll speak to Frau Chef.' And she added, with her music-hall grimace, 'He was probably counting your eyelashes.'

I returned to my room. Herr Stroh still sat in position, the field-glasses in his hands resting on his knees. As soon as I came within view, he raised the glasses to his eyes. I decided to stare him out until such time as Frau Lublonitsch should return and take the matter in hand.

For nearly an hour I sat patiently at the window. Herr Stroh rested his arms now and again, but he did not leave his seat. I could see him clearly, although I think I imagined the grin on his face as, from time to time, he raised the glasses to his eyes. There was no doubt that he could see, as if it were within an inch of his face, the fury on mine. It was too late now for one of us to give in, and I kept glancing down at the entrances to the Hotel Stroh, expecting to see Frau Lublonitsch or perhaps one of her sons or the yard hands going across to deliver a protest. But no one from our side approached the Stroh premises, from either the front or the back of the house. I continued to stare, and Herr Stroh continued to goggle through his glasses.

Then he dropped them. It was as if they had been jerked out of his hands by an invisible nudge. He approached close to the window and gazed, but now he was gazing at a point above and slightly to the left of my room. After about two minutes, he turned and disappeared.

Just then Gertha knocked at my door. 'Frau Chef has protested, and you won't have any more trouble,' she said.

'Did she telephone to his house?'

'No, Frau Chef doesn't use the phone; it mixes her up.'

'Who protested, then?'

'Frau Chef.'

'But she hasn't been across to see him. I've been watching the house.'

'No, Frau Chef doesn't visit with him. But don't worry, he knows all right that he mustn't annoy our guests.'

When I looked out of the window again, I saw that the blind of Herr Stroh's room had been pulled down, and so it remained for the rest of my stay.

Meantime, I went out to post my letters in the box opposite our hotel, across the path. The sun had come out more strongly, and Herr Stroh stood in his doorway blinking up at the roof of the Guesthouse Lublonitsch. He was engrossed, he did not notice me at all.

I didn't want to draw his attention by following the line of his gaze but I was curious as to what held him staring so trancelike up at our roof. On my way back from the postbox I saw what it was.

Like most of the roofs in that province, the Lublonitsch roof had a railed ledge running several inches above the eaves, for the purpose of preventing the snow from falling in heavy thumps during the winter. On this ledge, just below an attic window, stood the gold-and-rose ormolu clock that I had seen in Frau Lublonitsch's splendid bedroom.

I turned the corner just as Herr Stroh gave up his gazing; he went indoors, sullen and bent. Two car-loads of people who had moved into the hotel that morning were now moving out, shifting their baggage with speed and the signs of a glad departure. I knew that his house was nearly empty.

Before supper, I walked past the Hotel Stroh and down across the bridge to the café. There were no other customers in the place. The proprietor brought the harsh gin that was the local speciality over to my usual table and I sipped it while I waited for someone to come. I did not have to wait long, for two local women came in and ordered ices, as many of them did on their way home from work in the village shops. They held the long spoons in their rough, knobbly hands and talked, while the owner of the café came and sat with them to exchange the news of the day.

'Herr Stroh has been defying Frau Lublonitsch,' one of the women said.

'Not again?'

'He's been offending her tourists.'

'Dirty old Peeping Tom.'

'He only does it to annoy Frau Lublonitsch.'

'I saw the clock on the roof. I saw – '

'Stroh is finished, he – '

'Which clock?'

'What she bought from him last winter when he was hard up. All red and gold, like an altarpiece. A beautiful clock – it was his grandfather's when things were different.'

'Stroh is finished. She'll have his hotel. She'll have – '

'She'll have the pants off him.'

'He'll have to go. She'll get the place at her price. Then she'll build down to the bridge. Just wait and see. Next winter she'll have the Hotel Stroh. Last winter she had the clock. It's two years since she gave him the mortgage.'

'It's only Stroh's place that's standing in her way. She'll pull it down.'

The faces of the two women and the man nearly met across the café table, hypnotized by the central idea of their talk. The women's spoons rose to their mouths and returned to their ices while the man clasped his hands on the table in front of him. Their voices went on like a litany.

'She'll expand down to the bridge.'

'Perhaps beyond the bridge.'

'No, no, the bridge will be enough. She's not so young.'

'Poor old Stroh!'

'Why doesn't she expand in the other direction?'

'Because there isn't so much trade in the other direction.'

'The business is down here, this side of the river.'

'Old Stroh is upset.'

'She'll build down to the bridge. She'll pull down his place and build.'

'Beyond the bridge.'

'Old Stroh. His clock stuck up there for everyone to see.'

'What does he expect, the lazy old pig?'

'What does he expect to see with his field-glasses?'

'The tourists.'

'I wish him joy of the tourists.'

They giggled, then noticed me sitting within earshot, and came out of their trance.

How delicately Frau Lublonitsch had sent her deadly message! The ormolu clock was still there on the roof ledge when I returned. It was thus she had told him that time was passing and the end of summer was near, and that this hotel, like his clock, would soon be hers. As I passed, Herr Stroh shuffled out to his front door, rather drunk. He did not see me. He was looking at the clock where it hung in the sunset, he looked up at it as did the quaking enemies of the Lord upon the head of Holofernes. I wondered if the poor man would even live another winter; certainly he had taken his last feeble stand against Frau Lublonitsch.

As for her, she would probably live till she was ninety or more. The general estimate of her age was fifty-three, fifty-four, five, six: a healthy woman.

*

Next day, the clock was gone. Enough was enough. It had gone back to that glamorous room behind the kitchen to which Frau Lublonitsch retired in the early hours of the morning to think up her high conceptions, not lying supine like a defeated creature but propped up on the white pillows, surrounded by her crimson, her scarlet, her gold-and-rosy tints, which, like a religious discipline, disturbed her spirit out of its sloth. It was from here she planted the palm tree and built the shops.

When, next morning, I saw her scouring the pots in the yard and plodding about in her boots among the vegetables, I was somewhat terrified. She could have adorned her own person in scarlet and gold, she could have lived in a turreted mansion rivalling that of the apothecary in the village. But like one averting the evil eye or like one practising a pure disinterested art, she had stuck to her brown apron and her boots. And she would, without a doubt, have her reward. She would take the Hotel Stroh. She would march on the bridge, and beyond it. The café would be hers, the swimming pool, the cinema. All the market place would be hers before she died in the scarlet bed under the gold-fringed canopy, facing her ormolu clock, her deed-boxes, and her ineffectual bottle of medicine.

Almost as if they knew it, the three tourists remaining in the Hotel Stroh came over to inquire of Frau Lublonitsch if there were any rooms available and what her terms were. Her terms were modest, and she found room for two of them. The third left on his motorcycle that night.

Everyone likes to be on the winning side. I saw the two new arrivals from the Hotel Stroh sitting secure under the Lublonitsch chestnut tree, taking breakfast, next morning. Herr Stroh, more sober than before, stood watching the scene from his doorway. I thought, Why doesn't he spit on us, he's got nothing to lose? I saw again, in my mind's eye the ormolu clock set high in the sunset splendour. But I had

91

not yet got over my fury with him for spying into my room, and was moved, all in one stroke, with high contempt and deep pity, feverish triumph and chilly fear.

The Leaf-Sweeper

Behind the town hall there is a wooded parkland which, towards the end of November, begins to draw a thin blue cloud right into itself; and as a rule the park floats in this haze until mid-February. I pass every day, and see Johnnie Geddes in the heart of this mist, sweeping up the leaves. Now and again he stops, and jerking his long head erect, looks indignantly at the pile of leaves, as if it ought not to be there; then he sweeps on. This business of leaf-sweeping he learnt during the years he spent in the asylum; it was the job they always gave him to do; and when he was discharged the town council gave him the leaves to sweep. But the indignant movement of the head comes naturally to him, for this has been one of his habits since he was the most promising and buoyant and vociferous graduate of his year. He looks much older than he is, for it is not quite twenty years ago that Johnnie founded the Society for the Abolition of Christmas.

Johnnie was living with his aunt then. I was at school, and in the Christmas holidays Miss Geddes gave me her nephew's pamphlet, *How to Grow Rich at Christmas*. It sounded very likely, but it turned out that you grow rich at Christmas by doing away with Christmas, and so pondered Johnnie's pamphlet no further.

But it was only his first attempt. He had, within the next three years, founded his society of Abolitionists. His new book, *Abolish Christmas or We Die*, was in great demand at the public library, and my turn for it came at last. Johnnie was really convincing, this time, and most people were completely won over until after they had closed the book. I got an old copy for sixpence the other day, and despite the lapse of time it still proves conclusively that Christmas is a national crime. Johnnie demonstrates that every human-unit in the kingdom faces inevitable starvation within a period inversely proportional to that in which one in every six industrial-productivity units, if you see what he means, stops producing toys to fill the stockings of the educational-intake units. He cites appalling statistics to show that $1 \cdot 024$ per cent of the time squandered each Christmas in reckless shopping and thoughtless churchgoing brings the nation closer to its doom by five years. A few readers protested, but Johnnie was able to demolish their muddled arguments, and meanwhile the Society for the Abolition of Christmas increased. But Johnnie was troubled. Not only did Christmas rage throughout the kingdom as usual that year, but he had private information that many of the Society's members had broken the Oath of Abstention.

He decided, then, to strike at the very roots of Christmas. Johnnie gave up his job on the Drainage Supply Board; he gave up all his prospects, and, financed by a few supporters, retreated for two years to study the roots of Christmas. Then, all jubilant, Johnnie produced his next and last book, in which he established, either that Christmas was an invention of the Early Fathers to propitiate the pagans, or it was invented by the pagans to placate the Early Fathers, I forget which. Against the advice of his friends, Johnnie entitled it *Christmas and Christianity*. It sold eighteen copies. Johnnie never really recovered from this; and it happened, about that time, that the girl he was engaged to, an ardent Abolitionist, sent him a pullover she had knitted, for Christmas; he sent it back, enclosing a copy of the Society's rules, and she sent back the ring. But in any case, during Johnnie's absence, the Society had been undermined by a moderate·faction. These moderates finally became more moderate, and the whole thing broke up.

Soon after this, I left the district, and it was some years before I saw Johnnie again. One Sunday afternoon in summer, I was idling among the crowds who were gathered to hear the speakers at Hyde Park. One little crowd surrounded a man who bore a banner marked 'Crusade against Christmas'; his voice was frightening; it carried an unusually long way. This was Johnnie. A man in the crowd told me Johnnie was there every Sunday, very violent about Christmas, and that he would soon be taken up for insulting language. As I saw in the papers, he was soon taken up for insulting language. And a few months later I heard that poor Johnnie was in a mental home, because he had Christmas on the brain and couldn't stop shouting about it.

After that I forgot all about him until three years ago, in December, I went to live near the town where Johnnie had spent his youth. On the afternoon of Christmas Eve I was walking with a friend, noticing what had changed in my absence, and what hadn't. We passed a long, large house, once famous for its armoury, and I saw that the iron gates were wide open.

'They used to be kept shut,' I said.

'That's an asylum now,' said my friend; 'they let the mild cases work in the grounds, and leave the gates open to give them a feeling of freedom.'

'But,' said my friend, 'they lock everything inside. Door after door. The lift as well; they keep it locked.'

While my friend was chattering, I stood in the gateway and looked in. Just beyond the gate was a great bare elmtree. There I saw a man in brown corduroys, sweeping up the leaves. Poor soul, he was shouting about Christmas.

'That's Johnnie Geddes,' I said. 'Has he been here all these years?'

'Yes,' said my friend as we walked on. 'I believe he gets worse at this time of year.'

'Does his aunt see him?'

'Yes. And she sees nobody else.'

We were, in fact, approaching the house where Miss Geddes lived. I suggested we call on her. I had known her well.

'No fear,' said my friend.

I decided to go in, all the same, and my friend walked on to the town.

Miss Geddes had changed, more than the landscape. She had been a solemn, calm woman, and now she moved about quickly, and gave short agitated smiles. She took me to her sitting-room, and as she opened the door she called to someone inside.

'Johnnie, see who's come to see us!'

A man, dressed in a dark suit, was standing on a chair, fixing holly behind a picture. He jumped down.

'Happy Christmas,' he said. 'A Happy and a Merry Christmas indeed. I do hope,' he said, 'you're going to stay for tea, as we've got a delightful Christmas cake, and at this season of goodwill I would be cheered indeed if you could see how charmingly it's decorated; it has "Happy Christmas" in red icing, and then there's a robin and . . .'

'Johnnie,' said Miss Geddes, 'you're forgetting the carols.'

'The carols,' he said. He lifted a gramophone record from a pile and put it on. It was *The Holly and the Ivy*.

'It's *The Holly and the Ivy*,' said Miss Geddes. 'Can't we have something else? We had that all morning.'

'It is sublime,' he said, beaming from his chair, and holding up his hand for silence.

While Miss Geddes went to fetch the tea, and he sat absorbed in his carol, I watched him. He was so like Johnnie, that if I hadn't seen poor Johnnie a few moments before, sweeping up the asylum leaves, I would have thought he really was Johnnie. Miss Geddes returned with the tray, and while he rose to put on another record, he said something that startled me.

'I saw you in the crowd that Sunday when I was speaking at Hyde Park.'

'What a memory you have!' said Miss Geddes.

'It must be ten years ago,' he said.

'My nephew has altered his opinion of Christmas,' she explained. 'He always comes home for Christmas now, and don't we have a jolly time, Johnnie?'

'Rather!' he said. 'Oh, let me cut the cake.'

He was very excited about the cake. With a flourish he dug a large knife into the side. The knife slipped, and I saw it run deep into his finger. Miss Geddes did not move. He wrenched his cut finger away, and went on slicing the cake.

'Isn't it bleeding?' I said.

He held up his hand. I could see the deep cut, but there was no blood.

Deliberately, and perhaps desperately, I turned to Miss Geddes.

'That house up the road,' I said, 'I see it's a mental home now. I passed it this afternoon.'

'Johnnie,' said Miss Geddes, as one who knows the game is up, 'go and fetch the mince-pies.'

He went, whistling a carol.

'You passed the asylum,' said Miss Geddes wearily.

'Yes,' I said.

'And you saw Johnnie sweeping up the leaves.'

'Yes.'

We could still hear the whistling of the carol.

'Who is *he*?' I said.

'That's Johnnie's ghost,' she said. 'He comes home every Christmas.'

'But,' she said, 'I don't like him. I can't bear him any longer, and I'm going away tomorrow. I don't want Johnnie's ghost, I want Johnnie in flesh and blood.'

I shuddered, thinking of the cut finger that could not bleed. And I left, before Johnnie's ghost returned with the mince-pies.

Next day, as I had arranged to join a family who lived in the town, I started walking over about noon. Because of the light mist, I didn't see at first who it was approaching. It was a man, waving his arm to me. It turned out to be Johnnie's ghost.

'Happy Christmas. What do you think,' said Johnnie's ghost, 'my aunt has gone to London. Fancy, on Christmas day, and I thought she was at church, and here I am without anyone to spend a jolly Christmas with, and, of course, I forgive her, as it's the season of goodwill, but I'm glad to see you, because now I can come with you, wherever it is you're going, and we can all have a Happy . . .'

'Go away,' I said, and walked on.

It sounds hard. But perhaps you don't know how repulsive and loathsome is the ghost of a living man. The ghosts of the dead may be all right, but the ghost of mad Johnnie gave me the creeps.

'Clear off,' I said.

He continued walking beside me. 'As it's the time of goodwill, I make allowances for your tone,' he said. 'But I'm coming.'

We had reached the asylum gates, and there, in the grounds, I saw Johnnie sweeping the leaves. I suppose it was his way of going on strike, working on Christmas day. He was making a noise about Christmas.

On a sudden impulse I said to Johnnie's ghost, 'You want company?'

'Certainly,' he replied. 'It's the season of . . .'

'Then you shall have it,' I said.

I stood in the gateway. 'Oh, Johnnie,' I called.

He looked up.

'I've brought your ghost to see you, Johnnie.'

'Well, well,' said Johnnie, advancing to meet his ghost, 'Just imagine it!'

'Happy Christmas,' said Johnnie's ghost.

'Oh, really?' said Johnnie.

I left them to it. And when I looked back, wondering if they would come to blows, I saw that Johnnie's ghost was sweeping the leaves as well. They seemed to be arguing at the same time. But it was still misty, and really, I can't say whether, when I looked a second time, there were two men or one man sweeping the leaves.

Johnnie began to improve in the New Year. At least, he stopped shouting about Christmas, and then he never mentioned it at all; in a few months, when he had almost stopped saying anything, they discharged him.

The town council gave him the leaves of the park to sweep. He seldom speaks, and recognizes nobody. I see him every day at the late end of the year, working within the mist. Sometimes, if there is a sudden gust, he jerks his head up to watch a few leaves falling behind him, as if amazed that they are undeniably there, although, by rights, the falling of leaves should be stopped.

Coming to the edge of the lake we paused to look at our reflections in the water. It was then I recognized her from the past, her face looking up from the lake. She had not stopped talking.

I put on my dark glasses to shield my eyes from the sun and conceal my recognition from her eyes.

'Am I boring you?' she said.

'No, not a bit, Dr Gray.'

'Sure?'

It is discouraging to put on sun glasses in the middle of someone's intimate story. But they were necessary, now that I had recognized her, and was excited, and could only honourably hear what she had to say from a point of concealment.

'Must you wear those glasses?'

'Well, yes. The glare.'

'The wearing of dark glasses,' she said, 'is a modern psychological phenomenon. It signifies the trend towards impersonalization, the weapon of the modern Inquisitor, it – '

'There's a lot in what you say.' But I did not remove my glasses, for I had not asked for her company in the first place, and there is a limit to what one can listen to with the naked eye.

We walked round the new concrete verge of the old lake, and she continued the story of how she was led to give up general medical practice and take up psychology; and I looked at her, as she spoke, through my dark glasses, and because of the softening effect these have upon things I saw her again as I had seen her looking up from the lake, and again as in my childhood.

At the end of the thirties Leesden End was an L-shaped town. Our house stood near the top of the L. At the other extreme was the market. Mr Simmonds, the oculist, had his shop on the horizontal leg, and he lived there above the shop with his mother and sister. All the other shops in the row were attached to each other, but Mr Simmonds' stood apart, like a real house, with a lane on either side.

I was sent to have my eyes tested. He took me into the darkened interior and said, 'Sit down, dear.' He put his arm round my shoulder. His forefinger moved up and down on my neck. I was thirteen and didn't like to be rude to him. Dorothy Simmonds, his sister, came downstairs just then; she came upon us silently and dressed in a white overall. Before she had crossed the room to switch on a dim light Mr Simmonds removed his arm from my shoulder with such a jerk that I knew for certain he had not placed it there in innocence.

I had seen Miss Simmonds once before, at a garden fête, where she stood on a platform in a big hat and blue dress, and sang 'Sometimes between long shadows on the grass', while I picked up windfall apples, all of which seemed to be rotten. Now in her white overall she turned and gave me a hostile look, as if I had been seducing her brother. I felt sexually in the wrong, and started looking round the dark room with a wide-eyed air.

'Can you read?' said Mr Simmonds.

I stopped looking round. I said, 'Read what?' – for I had been told I would be asked to read row after row of letters. The card which hung beneath the dim light showed pictures of trains and animals.

'Because if you can't read we have pictures for illiterates.'

This was Mr Simmonds' joke. I giggled. His sister smiled

101

and dabbed her right eye with her handkerchief. She had been to London for an operation on her right eye.

I recall reading the letters correctly down to the last few lines, which were too small. I recall Mr Simmonds squeezing my arm as I left the shop, turning his sandy freckled face in a backward glance to see for certain that his sister was not watching.

My grandmother said, 'Did you see – '

' – Mr Simmonds' sister?' said my aunt.

'Yes, she was there all the time,' I said, to make it definite.

My grandmother said, 'They say she's going – '

' – blind in one eye,' said my aunt.

'And with the mother bedridden upstairs – ' my grandmother said.

' – she must be a saint,' said my aunt.

Presently – it may have been within a few days or a few weeks – my reading glasses arrived, and I wore them whenever I remembered to do so.

I broke the glasses by sitting on them during my school holidays two years later.

My grandmother said, after she had sighed, 'It's time you had your eyes tested – '

' – eyes tested in any case,' said my aunt when she had sighed.

I washed my hair the night before and put a wave in it. Next morning at eleven I walked down to Mr Simmonds' with one of my grandmother's long hat-pins in my blazer pocket. The shop front had been done up, with gold lettering on the glass door; Basil Simmonds, Optician, followed by a string of letters which, so far as I remember, were F.B.O.A., A.I.C., and others.

'You're quite the young lady, Joan,' he said, looking at my new breasts.

I smiled and put my hand in my blazer pocket.

He was smaller than he had been two years ago. I thought he must be about fifty or thirty. His face was more freckled than ever and his eyes were flat blue as from a box of paints. Miss Simmonds appeared silently in her soft slippers. 'You're quite the young lady, Joan,' she said from behind her green glasses, for her right eye had now gone blind and the other was said to be troubling her.

We went into the examination room. She glided past me and switched on the dim light above the letter card. I began to read out the letters while Basil Simmonds stood with folded hands. Someone came into the front shop. Miss Simmonds slid off to see who it was and her brother tickled my neck. I read on. He drew me towards him. I put my hand into my blazer pocket. He said, 'Oh!' and sprang away as the hat-pin struck through my blazer and into his thigh.

Miss Simmonds appeared in the doorway in her avenging white overall. Her brother, who had been rubbing his thigh in a puzzled way, pretended to be dusting a mark off the front of his trousers.

'What's wrong? Why did you shout?' she said.

'No, I didn't shout.'

She looked at me, then returned to attend to the person in the shop, leaving the intervening door wide open. She was back again almost immediately. My examination was soon over. Mr Simmonds saw me out at the front door and gave me a pleading unhappy look. I felt like a traitor and I considered him horrible.

For the rest of the holidays I thought of him as 'Basil', and by asking questions and taking more interest than usual in the conversation around me I formed an idea of his private life. 'Dorothy,' I speculated, 'and Basil.' I let my mind dwell on them until I saw a picture of the rooms above the shop. I hung round at tea-time and, in order to bring the conversation round to Dorothy and Basil, told our visitors I had been to get my eyes tested.

'The mother bedridden all these years and worth a fortune. But what good is it to her?'

'What chance is there for Miss Simmonds now, with that eye?'

'She'll get the money. He will get the bare legal minimum only.'

'No, they say he's to get everything. In trust.'

'I believe Mrs Simmonds has left everything to her daughter.'

My grandmother said, 'She should divide her fortune – '

' – equally between them,' said my aunt. 'Fair's fair.'

I invented for myself a recurrent scene in which brother and sister emerged from their mother's room and, on the narrow landing, allowed their gaze to meet in unspoken combat over their inheritance. Basil's flat-coloured eyes did not themselves hold any expression, but by the forward thrust of his red neck he indicated his meaning; Dorothy made herself plain by means of a corkscrew twist of the head – round and up – and the glitter of her one good eye through the green glasses.

I was sent for to try on my new reading glasses. I had the hat-pin with me. I was friendly to Basil while I tested the new glasses in the front shop. He seemed to want to put a hand on my shoulder, hovered, but was afraid. Dorothy came downstairs and appeared before us just as his hand wavered. He protracted the wavering gesture into one which adjusted the stem of my glasses above my ear.

'Auntie says to try them properly,' I said, 'while I'm about it.' This gave me an opportunity to have a look round the front premises.

'You'll only want them for your studies,' Basil said.

'Oh, I sometimes need glasses even when I'm not

104

reading.' I said. I was looking through a door into a small inner office, darkened by a tree outside in the lane. The office contained a dumpy green safe, an old typewriter on a table, and a desk in the window with a ledger on it. Other ledgers were placed –

'Nonsense,' Dorothy was saying. 'A healthy girl like you – you hardly need glasses at all. For reading, to save your eyes, perhaps *yes*. But when you're not reading . . .'

I said 'Grandmother said to enquire after your mother.'

'She's failing,' she said.

I took to giving Basil a charming smile when I passed him in the street on the way to the shops. This was very frequently. And on these occasions he would be standing at his shop door awaiting my return; then I would snub him. I wondered how often he was prepared to be won and rejected within the same ten minutes.

I took walks before supper round the back lanes, ambling right round the Simmonds' house, thinking of what was going on inside. One dusky time it started to rain heavily, and I found I could reasonably take shelter under the tree which grew quite close to the grimy window of the inner office. I could just see over the ledge and make out a shape of a person sitting at the desk. Soon, I thought, the shape will have to put on the light.

After five minutes' long waiting time the shape arose and switched on the light by the door. It was Basil, suddenly looking pink-haired. As he returned to the desk he stooped and took from the safe a sheaf of papers held in the teeth of a large paper clip. I knew he was going to select one sheet of paper from the sheaf, and that this one document would be the exciting, important one. It was like reading a familiar book: one knew what was coming, but couldn't bear to miss a word. He did extract one long sheet of paper, and held it up. It was typewritten with a paragraph in handwriting at the bottom on the side visible from the window. He laid it side by side with another sheet of paper which was lying on the desk. I pressed close up to the window, intending to wave and smile if I was seen, and to call out that I was sheltering from the rain which was now coming down in thumps. But he kept his eyes on the two sheets of paper. There were other papers lying about the desk; I could not see what was on them. But I was quite convinced that he had been practising handwriting on them, and that he was in the process of forging his mother's will.

Then he took up the pen. I can still smell the rain and hear it thundering about me, and feel it dripping on my head from the bough overhanging above me. He raised his eyes and looked out at the rain. It seemed his eyes rested on me, at my station between the tree and the window. I kept still and close to the tree like a hunted piece of nature, willing myself to be the colour of bark and leaves and rain. Then I realized how much more clearly I could see him than he me, for it was growing dark.

He pulled a sheet of blotting paper towards him. He dipped his pen in the ink and started writing on the bottom of the sheet of paper before him, comparing it from time to time with the one he had taken out of the safe. I was not surprised, but I was thrilled, when the door behind him slowly opened. It was like seeing the film of the book. Dorothy advanced on her creeping feet, and he did not hear, but formed the words he was writing, on and on. The rain pelted down regardless. She was looking crookedly, through her green glasses with her one eye, over his shoulder at the paper.

'What are you doing?' she said.

He jumped up and pulled the blotting paper over his work. Her one eye through her green glasses glinted upon him, though I did not actually see it do so, but saw only the dark green glass focused with a squint on to his face.

'I'm making up the accounts,' he said, standing with his

back to the desk, concealing the papers. I saw his hand reach back and tremble among them.

I shivered in my soaking wet clothes. Dorothy looked with her eye at the window. I slid sideways to avoid her and ran all the way home.

Next morning I said, 'I've tried to read with these glasses. It's all a blur. I suppose I'll *have* to take them back?'

'Didn't you notice anything wrong when you tried – '

' – tried them on in the shop?'

'No. But the shop's so dark. *Must* I take them back?'

I took them into Mr Simmonds early that afternoon.

'I tried to read with them this morning, but it's all a blur.' It was true that I had smeared them with cold cream first.

Dorothy was beside us in no time. She peered one-eyed at the glasses, then at me.

'Are you constipated?' she said.

I maintained silence. But I felt she was seeing everything through her green glasses.

'Put them on,' Dorothy said.

'Try them on,' said Basil.

They were ganged up together. Everything was going wrong, for I had come here to see how matters stood between them after the affair of the will.

Basil gave me something to read, 'It's all right now,' I said, 'but it was all a blur when I tried to read this morning.'

'Better take a dose,' Dorothy said.

I wanted to get out of the shop with my glasses as quickly as possible, but the brother said, 'I'd better test your eyes again while you're here just to make sure.'

He seemed quite normal. I followed him into the dark interior. Dorothy switched on the light. They both seemed normal. The scene in the little office last night began to lose its conviction. As I read out the letters on the card in front of me I was thinking of Basil as 'Mr Simmonds' and Dorothy as 'Miss Simmonds', and feared their authority, and was in the wrong.

'That seems to be all right,' Mr Simmonds said. 'But wait a moment.' He produced some coloured slides with lettering on them.

Miss Simmonds gave me what appeared to be a triumphant one-eyed leer, and as one who washes her hands of a person, started to climb the stairs. Plainly, she knew I had lost my attraction for her brother.

But before she turned the bend in the stairs she stopped and came down again. She went to a row of shelves and shifted some bottles. I read on. She interrupted;

'My eye-drops, Basil. I made them up this morning. Where are they?'

Mr Simmonds was suddenly watching her as if something inconceivable was happening.

'Wait, Dorothy. Wait till I've tested the girl's eyes.'

She had lifted down a small brown bottle. 'I want my eye-drops. I wish you wouldn't displace. Are – these they?'

I noted her correct phrase, 'Are these they?' and it seemed just over the border of correctness. Perhaps, after all, this brother and sister were strange, vicious, in the wrong.

She had raised the bottle and was reading the label with her one good eye. 'Yes, this is mine. It has my name on it,' she said.

Dark Basil, dark Dorothy. There was something wrong after all. She walked upstairs with her bottle of eye-drops. The brother put his hand on my elbow and heaved me to my feet, forgetting his coloured slides.

'There's nothing wrong with your eyes. Off you go.' He pushed me into the front shop. His flat eyes were wide open as he handed me my glasses. He pointed to the door. 'I'm a busy man,' he said.

From upstairs came a long scream. Basil jerked open the door for me, but I did not move. Then Dorothy, upstairs, screamed and screamed and screamed. Basil put his hands to his head, covering his eyes. Dorothy appeared on the bend of the stairs, screaming, doubled-up, with both hands covering her good eye.

I started screaming when I got home, and was given a sedative. By evening everyone knew that Miss Simmonds had put the wrong drops in her eyes.

'Will she go blind in that eye, too?' people said.

'The doctor says there's hope.'

'There will be an enquiry.'

'She was going blind in that eye in any case,' they said.

'Ah, but the pain . . .'

'Whose mistake, hers or his?'

'Joan was there at the time. Joan heard the screams. We had to give her a sedative to calm – '

' – calm her down.'

'But who made the mistake?'

'She usually makes up the eye-drops herself. She's got a dispenser's – '

' – dispenser's certificate, you know.'

'Her name was on the bottle, Joan says.'

'Who wrote the name on the bottle? That's the question. They'll find out from the handwriting. If it was Mr Simmonds he'll be disqualified.'

'She always wrote the names on the bottles. She'll be put off the dispensers' roll, poor thing.'

'They'll lose their licence.'

'I got eye-drops from them myself only three weeks ago. If I'd have known what I know now, I'd never have – '

'The doctor says they can't find the bottle, it's got lost.'

'No, the sergeant says definitely they've got the bottle. The handwriting is hers. She must have made up the drops herself, poor thing.'

'Deadly nightshade, same thing.'

'Stuff called atropine. Belladonna. Deadly nightshade.'

'It should have been stuff called eserine. That's what she usually had, the doctor says.'

'Dr *Gray* says?'

'Yes, Dr Gray.'

'Dr Gray says if you switch from eserine to atropine – '

It was put down to an accident. There was a strong hope that Miss Simmonds' one eye would survive. It was she who had made up the prescription. She refused to discuss it.

I said, 'The bottle may have been tampered with, have you thought of that?'

'Joan's been reading books.'

The last week of my holidays old Mrs Simmonds died above the shop and left all her fortune to her daughter. At the same time I got tonsillitis and could not return to school.

I was attended by our woman doctor, the widow of the town's former doctor who had quite recently died. This was the first time I had seen Dr Gray, although I had known the other Dr Gray, her husband, whom I missed. The new Dr Gray was a sharp-faced athletic woman. She was said to be young. She came to visit me every day for a week. After consideration I decided she was normal and in the right, though dull.

Through the feverish part of my illness I saw Basil at the desk through the window and I heard Dorothy scream. While I was convalescent I went for walks, and always returned by the lane beside the Simmonds' house. There had been no bickering over the mother's will. Everyone said the eye-drop affair was a terrible accident. Miss Simmonds had retired and was said to be going rather dotty.

I saw Dr Gray leaving the Simmonds' at six o'clock one evening. She must have been calling on poor Miss Simmonds. She noticed me at once as I emerged from the lane.

'Don't loiter about, Joan. It's getting chilly.'

The next evening I saw a light in the office window. I stood under the tree and looked. Dr Gray sat upon the desk with her back to me, quite close. Mr Simmonds sat in his chair talking to her, tilting back his chair. A bottle of sherry stood on the table. They each had a glass half-filled with sherry. Dr Gray swung her legs, she was in the wrong, sexy, like our morning help who sat on the kitchen table swinging her legs.

But then she spoke. 'It will take time,' she said. 'A very difficult patient, of course.'

Basil nodded. Dr Gray swung her legs, and looked professional. She was in the right, she looked like our games mistress who sometimes sat on a desk swinging her legs.

Before I returned to school I saw Basil one morning at his shop door. 'Reading glasses all right now?' he said.

'Oh yes, thank you.'

'There's nothing wrong with your sight. Don't let your imagination run away with you.'

I walked on, certain that he had known my guilty suspicions all along.

'I took up psychology during the war. Up till then I was in general practice.'

I had come to the summer school to lecture on history and she on psychology. Psychiatrists are very often ready to talk to strangers about their inmost lives. This is probably because they spend so much time hearing out their patients. I did not recognize Dr Gray, except as a type, when I had attended her first lecture on 'the psychic manifestations of sex'. She spoke of child-poltergeists, and I was bored, and took refuge in observing the curious language of her profession. I noticed the word 'arousement'. 'Adolescents in a state of sexual arousement,' she said, 'may become possessed of almost psychic insight.'

111

After lunch, since the Eng. Lit. people had gone off to play tennis, she tacked on to me and we walked to the lake across the lawns, past the rhododendrons. This lake had once been the scene of a love-mad duchess's death.

'. . . during the war. Before that I was in general practice. It's strange,' she said, 'how I came to take up psychology. My second husband had a breakdown and was under a psychiatrist. Of course, he's incurable, but I decided . . . It's strange, but that's how I came to take it up. It saved *my* reason. My husband is still in a home. His sister, of course, became quite incurable. *He* has his lucid moments. I did not realize it, of course, when I married, but there was what I'd now call an oedipus-transference on his part, and . . .'

How tedious I found these phrases! We had come to the lake. I stooped over it and myself looked back at myself through the dark water. I looked at Dr Gray's reflection and recognized her. I put on my dark glasses, then.

'Am I boring you?' she said.

'No, carry on.'

'Must you wear those glasses? . . . it is a modern psychological phenomenon . . . the trend towards impersonalization . . . the modern Inquisitor.'

For a while, she watched her own footsteps as we walked round the lake. Then she continued her story. ' . . . an optician. His sister was blind – *going* blind when I first attended her. Only the one eye was affected. Then there was an accident, one of those *psychological* accidents. She was a trained dispenser, but she mixed herself the wrong eye-drops. Now it's very difficult to make a mistake like that, normally. But subconsciously she wanted to, she *wanted* to. But she wasn't normal, she was not normal.'

'I'm not saying she was,' I said.

'What did you say?'

'I'm sure she wasn't a normal person,' I said, 'if you say so.'

'It can all be explained psychologically, as we've tried to show to my husband. We've told him and told him, and given him every sort of treatment – shock, insulin, everything. And after all, the stuff didn't have any effect on his sister immediately, and when she did go blind it was caused by acute glaucoma. She would probably have lost her sight in any case. Well, she went off her head completely and accused her brother of having put the wrong drug in the bottle deliberately. This is the interesting part from the psychological point of view – she said she had seen something that he didn't want her to see, something disreputable. She said he wanted to blind the eye that saw it. She said . . .'

We were walking round the lake for the second time. When we came to the spot where I had seen her face reflected I stopped and looked over the water.

'I'm boring you.'

'No, no.'

'I wish you would take off those glasses.'

I took them off for a moment. I rather liked her for her innocence in not recognizing me, though she looked hard and said, 'There's a subconscious reason why you wear them.'

'Dark glasses hide dark thoughts,' I said.

'Is that a saying?'

'Not that I've heard. But it is one now.'

She looked at me anew. But she didn't recognize me. These fishers of the mind have no eye for outward things. Instead, she was 'recognizing' my mind: I daresay I came under some category of hers.

I had my glasses on again, and was walking on.

'How did your husband react to his sister's accusations?' I said.

'He was remarkably kind.'

'Kind?'

113

'Oh, yes, in the circumstances. Because she started up a lot of gossip in the neighbourhood. It was only a small town. It was a long time before I could persuade him to send her to a home for the blind where she could be looked after. There was a terrible bond between them. Unconscious incest.'

'Didn't you know that when you married him? I should have thought it would have been obvious.'

She looked at me again. 'I had not studied psychology at that time,' she said.

I thought, neither had I.

We were silent for the third turn about the lake. Then she said, 'Well, I was telling you how I came to study psychology and practise it. My husband had this breakdown after his sister went away. He had delusions. He kept imagining he saw eyes looking at him everywhere. He still sees them from time to time. But *eyes*, you see. That's significant. Unconsciously he felt he had blinded his sister. Because unconsciously he wanted to do so. He keeps confessing that he did so.'

'And attempted to forge the will?' I said.

She stopped. 'What are you saying?'

'Does he admit that he tried to forge his mother's will?'

'I haven't mentioned anything about a will.'

'Oh, I thought you had.'

'But, in fact, that was his sister's accusation. What made you say that? How did you know?'

'I must be psychic,' I said.

She took my arm. I had become a most endearing case-history.

'You must be psychic indeed,' she said. 'You must tell me more about yourself. Well, that's the story of my taking up my present profession. When my husband started having these delusions and making these confessions I felt I had to understand the workings of the mind. And I began to study them. It has been fruitful. It has saved my own reason.'

'Did it ever occur to you that the sister's story might be true?' I said. 'Especially as he admits it.'

She took away her arm and said, 'Yes, I considered the possibility. I must admit I considered it well.'

She saw me watching her face. She looked as if she were pleading some personal excuse.

'Oh do,' she said, 'please take off those glasses.'

'Why don't you believe his own confession?'

'I'm a psychiatrist and we seldom believe confessions.' She looked at her watch as if to suggest I had started the whole conversation and was boring her.

I said, 'He might have stopped seeing eyes if you'd taken him at his word.'

She shouted, 'What are you saying? What are you thinking of? He wanted to give a statement to the police, do you realize . . .'

'You know he's guilty,' I said.

'As his wife,' she said, 'I know he's guilty. But as a psychiatrist I must regard him as innocent. That's why I took up the subject.' She suddenly turned angry and shouted, 'You damned inquisitor, I've met your type before.'

I could hardly believe she was shouting, who previously had been so calm. 'Oh, it's not my business,' I said, and took off my glasses to show willing.

I think it was then she recognized me.

The House of the Famous Poet

In the summer of 1944, when it was nothing for trains from the provinces to be five or six hours late, I travelled to London on the night train from Edinburgh, which, at York, was already three hours late. There were ten people in the compartment, only two of whom I remember well, and for good reason.

I have the impression, looking back on it, of a row of people opposite me, dozing untidily with heads askew, and, as it often seems when we look at sleeping strangers, their features had assumed extra emphasis and individuality, sometimes disturbing to watch. It was as if they had rendered up their daytime talent for obliterating the outward traces of themselves in exchange for mental obliteration. In this way they resembled a twelfth-century fresco; there was a look of medieval unselfconsciousness about these people, all except one.

This was a private soldier who was awake to a greater degree than most people are when they are not sleeping. He was smoking cigarettes one after the other with long, calm puffs. I thought he looked excessively evil – an atavistic type. His forehead must have been less than two inches high above dark, thick eyebrows, which met. His jaw was not large, but it was apelike; so was his small nose and so were his deep, close-set eyes. I thought there must have been some consanguinity in the parents. He was quite a throwback.

As it turned out, he was extremely gentle and kind. When I ran out of cigarettes, he fished about in his haversack and produced a packet for me and one for a girl sitting next to

116

me. We both tried, with a flutter of small change, to pay him. Nothing would please him at all but that we should accept his cigarettes, whereupon he returned to his silent, reflective smoking.

I felt a sort of pity for him then, rather as we feel towards animals we know to be harmless, such as monkeys. But I realized that, like the pity we expend on monkeys merely because they are not human beings, this pity was not needed.

Receiving the cigarettes gave the girl and myself common ground, and we conversed quietly for the rest of the journey. She told me she had a job in London as a domestic helper and nursemaid. She looked as if she had come from a country district – her very blonde hair, red face and large bones gave the impression of power, as if she was used to carrying heavy things, perhaps great scuttles of coal, or two children at a time. But what made me curious about her was her voice, which was cultivated, melodious and restrained.

Towards the end of the journey, when the people were beginning to jerk themselves straight and the rushing to and fro in the corridor had started, this girl, Elise, asked me to come with her to the house where she worked. The master, who was something in a university, was away with his wife and family.

I agreed to this, because at that time I was in the way of thinking that the discovery of an educated servant girl was valuable and something to be gone deeper into. It had the element of experience – perhaps, even of truth – and I believed, in those days, that truth is stranger than fiction. Besides, I wanted to spend that Sunday in London. I was due back next day at my job in a branch of the civil service, which had been evacuated to the country and for a reason that is another story, I didn't want to return too soon. I had some telephoning to do, I wanted to wash and change. I wanted to know more about the girl. So I thanked Elise and accepted her invitation.

I regretted it as soon as we got out of the train at King's Cross, some minutes after ten. Standing up tall on the platform, Elise looked unbearably tired, as if not only the last night's journey but every fragment of her unknown life was suddenly heaping up on top of her. The power I had noticed in the train was no longer there. As she called, in her beautiful voice, for a porter, I saw that on the side of her head that had been away from me in the train, her hair was parted in a dark streak, which, by contrast with the yellow, looked navy blue. I had thought, when I first saw her, that possibly her hair was bleached, but now, seeing it so badly done, seeing this navy blue parting pointing like an arrow to the weighted weariness of her face, I, too, got the sensation of great tiredness. And it was not only the strain of the journey that I felt, but the foreknowledge of boredom that comes upon us unaccountably at the beginning of a quest, and that checks, perhaps mercifully, our curiosity.

And, as it happened, there really wasn't much to learn about Elise. The explanation of her that I had been prompted to seek, I got in the taxi between King's Cross and the house at Swiss Cottage. She came of a good family, who thought her a pity, and she them. Having no training for anything else, she had taken a domestic job on leaving home. She was engaged to an Australian soldier billeted also at Swiss Cottage.

Perhaps it was the anticipation of a day's boredom, maybe it was the effect of no sleep or the fact that the V-1 sirens were sounding, but I felt some sourness when I saw the house. The garden was growing all over the place. Elise opened the front door, and we entered a darkish room almost wholly taken up with a long, plain wooden work-table. On this, were a half-empty marmalade jar, a pile of papers, and a dried-up ink bottle. There was a steel-

118

canopied bed, **known as a Morrison shelter**, in one corner and some photographs on the mantelpiece, one of a school-boy wearing glasses. Everything was tainted with Elise's weariness and my own distaste. But Elise didn't seem to be aware of the exhaustion so plainly revealed on her face. She did not even bother to take her coat off, and as it was too tight for her I wondered how she could move about so quickly with this restriction added to the weight of her tiredness. But, with her coat still buttoned tight Elise phoned her boy-friend and made breakfast, while I washed in a dim, blue, cracked bathroom upstairs.

When I found that she had opened my hold-all without asking me and had taken out my rations, I was a little pleased. It seemed a friendly action, with some measure of reality about it, and I felt better. But I was still irritated by the house. I felt there was no justification for the positive lack of consequence which was lying about here and there. I asked no questions about the owner who was something in a university, for fear of getting the answer I expected – that he was away visiting his grandchildren, at some family gathering in the home counties. The owners of the house had no reality for me, and I looked upon the place as belonging to, and permeated with, Elise.

I went with her to a nearby public house, where she met her boy-friend and one or two other Australian soldiers. They had with them a thin Cockney girl with bad teeth. Elise was very happy, and insisted in her lovely voice that they should all come along to a party at the house that evening. In a fine aristocratic tone, she demanded that each should bring a bottle of beer.

During the afternoon Elise said she was going to have a bath, and she showed me a room where I could use the telephone and sleep if I wanted. This was a large, light room with several windows, much more orderly than the rest of the house, and lined with books. There was only one unusual thing about it: beside one of the windows was a bed, but this bed was only a fairly thick mattress made up neatly on the floor. It was obviously a bed on the floor with some purpose, and again I was angered to think of the futile crankiness of the elderly professor who had thought of it.

I did my telephoning, and decided to rest. But first I wanted to find something to read. The books puzzled me. None of them seemed to be automatically part of a scholar's library. An inscription in one book was signed by the author, a well-known novelist. I found another inscribed copy, and this had the name of the recipient. On a sudden idea, I went to the desk, where while I had been telephoning I had noticed a pile of unopened letters. For the first time, I looked at the name of the owner of the house.

I ran to the bathroom and shouted through the door to Elise, 'Is this house of the famous poet?'

'Yes,' she called. 'I *told* you.'

She had told me nothing of the kind. I felt I had no right at all to be there, for it wasn't, now, the house of Elise acting by proxy for some unknown couple. It was the house of a famous modern poet. The thought that at any moment he and his family might walk in and find me there terrified me. I insisted that Elise should open the bathroom door and tell me to my face that there was no possible chance of their returning for many days to come.

Then I began to think about the house itself, which Elise was no longer accountable for. Its new definition, as the house of a poet whose work I knew well, many of whose poems I knew by heart, gave it altogether a new appearance.

To confirm this, I went outside and stood exactly where I had been when I first saw the garden from the door of the taxi. I wanted to get my first impression for a second time.

And this time I saw an absolute purpose in the overgrown garden, which, since then, I have come to believe existed in the eye of the beholder. But, at the time, the room we had first entered, and which had riled me, now began to give back a meaning, and whatever was, was right. The caked-up bottle of ink, which Elise had put on the mantel-piece, I replaced on the table to make sure. I saw a photograph I hadn't noticed before, and I recognized the famous poet.

It was the same with the upstairs room where Elise had put me, and I handled the books again, not so much with the sense that they belonged to the famous poet but with some curiosity about how they had been made. The sort of question that occurred to me was where the paper had come from and from what sort of vegetation was manufactured the black print, and these things have not troubled me since.

The Australians and the Cockney girl came around about seven. I had planned to catch an eight-thirty train to the country, but when I telephoned to confirm the time I found there were no Sunday trains running. Elise, in her friendly and exhausted way, begged me to stay without attempting to be too serious about it. The sirens were starting up again. I asked Elise once more to repeat that the poet and his family could by no means return that night. But I asked this question more abstractedly than before, as I was thinking of the sirens and of the exact proportions of the noise they made. I wondered, as well, what sinister genius of the Home Office could have invented so ominous a wail, and why. And I was thinking of the word 'siren'. The sound then became comical, for I imagined some maniac sea nymph from centuries past belching into the year 1944. Actually, the sirens frightened me.

Most of all, I wondered about Elise's party. Everyone roamed about the place as if it were nobody's house in particular, with Elise the best-behaved of the lot. The Cockney girl sat on the long table and gave of her best to the skies every time a bomb exploded. I had the feeling that the house had been requisitioned for an evening by the military. It was so hugely and everywhere occupied that it became not the house I had first entered, nor the house of the famous poet, but a third house – the one I had vaguely prefigured when I stood, bored, on the platform at King's Cross station. I saw a great amount of tiredness among these people, and heard, from the loud noise they made, that they were all lacking sleep. When the beer was finished and they were gone, some to their billets, some to pubs, and the Cockney girl to her Underground shelter where she had slept for weeks past, I asked Elise, 'Don't you feel tired?'

'No,' she said with agonizing weariness, 'I never feel tired.'

I fell asleep myself, as soon as I had got into the bed on the floor in the upstairs room, and overslept until Elise woke me at eight. I had wanted to get up early to catch a nine o'clock train, so I hadn't much time to speak to her. I did notice, though, that she had lost some of her tired look.

I was pushing my things into my hold-all while Elise went up the street to catch a taxi when I heard someone coming upstairs. I thought it was Elise come back, and I looked out of the open door. I saw a man in uniform carrying an enormous parcel in both hands. He looked down as he climbed, and had a cigarette in his mouth.

'Do you want Elise?' I called, thinking it was one of her friends.

He looked up, and I recognized the soldier, the throw-back, who had given us cigarettes in the train.

'Well, anyone will do,' he said. 'The thing is, I've got to get back to camp and I'm stuck for the fare – eight and six.'

I told him I could manage it, and was finding the money when he said, putting his parcel on the floor, 'I don't want to borrow it. I wouldn't think of borrowing it. I've got something for sale.'

'What's that?' I said.

'A funeral,' said the soldier. 'I've got it here.'

This alarmed me, and I went to the window. No hearse, no coffin stood below. I saw only the avenue of trees.

The soldier smiled. 'It's an abstract funeral,' he explained, opening the parcel.

He took it out and I examined it carefully, greatly comforted. It was very much the sort of thing I had wanted – rather more purple in parts than I would have liked, for I was not in favour of this colour of mourning. Still, I thought I could tone it down a bit.

Delighted with the bargain, I handed over the eight shillings and sixpence. There was a great deal of this abstract funeral. Hastily, I packed some of it into the holdall. Some I stuffed in my pockets, and there was still some left over. Elise had returned with a cab and I hadn't much time. So I ran for it, out of the door and out of the gate of the house of the famous poet, with the rest of my funeral trailing behind me.

You will complain that I am withholding evidence. Indeed, you may wonder if there is any evidence at all. 'An abstract funeral,' you will say, 'is neither here nor there. It is only a notion. You cannot pack a notion into your bag. You cannot see the colour of a notion.'

You will insinuate that what I have just told you is pure fiction.

Hear me to the end.

I caught the train. Imagine my surprise when I found, sitting opposite me, my friend the soldier, of whose existence you are so sceptical.

'As a matter of interest,' I said, 'how would you describe all this funeral you sold me?'

'Describe it?' he said. 'Nobody describes an abstract funeral. You just conceive it.'

'There is much in what you say,' I replied. 'Still, describe

123

it I must, because it is not every day one comes by an abstract funeral.'

'I am glad you appreciate that,' said the soldier.

'And after the war,' I continued, 'when I am no longer a civil servant, I hope, in a few deftly turned phrases, to write of my experiences at the house of the famous poet, which has culminated like this. But of course,' I added, 'I will need to say what it looks like.'

The soldier did not reply.

'If it were an okapi or a sea-cow,' I said, 'I would have to say what it looked like. No one would believe me otherwise.'

'Do you want your money back?' asked the soldier. 'Because if so, you can't have it. I spent it on my ticket.'

'Don't misunderstand me,' I hastened to say. 'The funeral is a delightful abstraction. Only, I wish to put it down in writing.'

I felt a great pity for the soldier on seeing his worried look. The apelike head seemed the saddest thing in the world.

'I make them by hand,' he said, 'these abstract funerals.'

A siren sounded somewhere, far away.

'Elise bought one of them last month. She hadn't any complaints. I change at the next stop,' he said, getting down his kit from the rack. 'And what's more,' he said, 'your famous poet bought one.'

'Oh, did he?' I said.

'Yes,' he said. 'No complaints. It was just what he wanted – the idea of a funeral.'

The train pulled up. The soldier leaped down and waved. As the train started again, I unpacked my abstract funeral and looked at it for a few moments.

'To hell with the idea,' I said. 'It's a real funeral I want.'

'All in good time,' said a voice from the corridor.

'*You* again,' I said. It was the soldier.

'No,' he said, 'I got off at the last station. I'm only a notion of myself.'

'Look here,' I said, 'would you be offended if I throw all this away?'

'Of course not,' said the soldier. 'You can't offend a notion.'

'I want a real funeral,' I explained. 'One of my own.'

'That's right,' said the soldier.

'And then I'll be able to write about it and go into all the details,' I said.

'Your own funeral?' he said. 'You want to write it up?'

'Yes,' I said.

'But,' said he, 'you're only human. Nobody reports on their own funeral. It's got to be abstract.'

'You see my predicament?' I said.

'I see it,' he replied. 'I get off at this stop.'

This notion of a soldier alighted. Once more the train put on speed. Out of the window I chucked all my eight and sixpence worth of abstract funeral. I watched it fluttering over the fields and around the tops of camouflaged factories with the sun glittering richly upon it, until it was out of sight.

In the summer of 1944 a great many people were harshly and suddenly killed. The papers reported, in due course, those whose names were known to the public. One of these, the famous poet, had returned unexpectedly to his home at Swiss Cottage a few moments before it was hit direct by a flying bomb. Fortunately, he had left his wife and children in the country.

When I got to the place where my job was, I had some time to spare before going on duty. I decided to ring Elise and thank her properly, as I had left in such a hurry. But the lines were out of order, and the operator could not find words enough to express her annoyance with me. Behind this overworked, quarrelsome voice from the exchange I

125

heard the high, long hoot which means that the telephone at the other end is not functioning, and the sound made me infinitely depressed and weary; it was more intolerable to me than the sirens, and I replaced the receiver; and, in fact, Elise had already perished under the house of the famous poet.

The blue cracked bathroom, the bed on the floor, the caked ink bottle, the neglected garden, and the neat rows of books – I try to gather them together in my mind whenever I am enraged by the thought that Elise and the poet were killed outright. The angels of the Resurrection will invoke the dead man and the dead woman, but who will care to restore the fallen house of the famous poet if not myself? Who else will tell its story?

When I reflect how Elise and the poet were taken in – how they calmly allowed a well-meaning soldier to sell them the notion of a funeral, I remind myself that one day I will accept, and so will you, an abstract funeral, and make no complaints.

A Member of the Family

'You must,' said Richard, suddenly, one day in November, 'come and meet my mother.'

Trudy, who had been waiting a long time for this invitation, after all was amazed.

'I should like you,' said Richard, 'to meet my mother. She's looking forward to it.'

'Oh, does she know about me?'

'Rather,' Richard said.

'Oh!'

'No need to be nervous,' Richard said. 'She's awfully sweet.'

'Oh, I'm sure she is. Yes, of course, I'd love – '

'Come to tea on Sunday,' he said.

They had met the previous June in a lake town in Southern Austria. Trudy had gone with a young woman who had a bed-sitting-room in Kensington just below Trudy's room. This young woman could speak German, whereas Trudy couldn't.

Bleilach was one of the cheaper lake towns; in fact, cheaper was a way of putting it: it was cheap.

'Gwen, I didn't realize it ever rained here,' Trudy said on their third day. 'It's all rather like Wales,' she said, standing by the closed double windows of their room regarding the downpour and imagining the mountains which indeed were there, but invisible.

'You said that yesterday,' Gwen said, 'and it was quite fine yesterday. Yesterday you said it was like Wales.'

'Well, it rained a bit yesterday.'

'But the sun was shining when you said it was like Wales.'

'Well, so it is.'

'On a much larger scale, I should say,' Gwen said.

'I didn't realize it would be so wet.' Then Trudy could almost hear Gwen counting twenty.

'You have to take your chance,' Gwen said. 'This is an unfortunate summer.'

The pelting of the rain increased as if in confirmation.

Trudy thought, I'd better shut up. But suicidally: 'Wouldn't it be better if we moved to a slightly more expensive place?' she said.

'The rain falls on the expensive places too. It falls on the just and the unjust alike.'

Gwen was thirty-five, a school teacher. She wore her hair and her clothes and her bit of lipstick in such a way that, standing by the window looking out at the rain, it occurred to Trudy like a revelation that Gwen had given up all thoughts of marriage. 'On the just and the unjust alike,' said Gwen, turning her maddening imperturbable eyes upon Trudy, as if to say, you are the unjust and I'm the just.

Next day was fine. They swam in the lake. They sat drinking apple juice under the red and yellow awnings on the terrace of their guesthouse and gazed at the innocent smiling mountain. They paraded – Gwen in her navy blue shorts and Trudy in her puffy sun-suit – along the lake-side where marched also the lean brown camping youths from all over the globe, the fat print-frocked mothers and double-chinned fathers from Germany followed by their blonde sedate young, and the English women with their perms.

'There aren't any men about,' Trudy said.

'There are hundreds of men,' Gwen said, in a voice which meant, whatever do you mean?

'I really must try out my phrase-book,' Trudy said, for she had the feeling that if she were independent of Gwen as interpreter she might, as she expressed it to herself, have more of a chance.

'You might have more of a chance of meeting someone interesting that way,' Gwen said, for their close confinement by the rain had seemed to make her psychic, and she was continually putting Trudy's thoughts into words.

'Oh, I'm not here for that. I only wanted a rest, as I told you. I'm not – '

'Goodness, Richard!'

Gwen was actually speaking English to a man who was not apparently accompanied by a wife or aunt or sister.

He kissed Gwen on the cheek. She laughed and so did he. 'Well, well,' he said. He was not much taller than Gwen. He had dark crinkly hair and a small moustache of a light brown. He wore bathing trunks and his large chest was impressively bronze. 'What brings you here?' he said to Gwen, looking meanwhile at Trudy.

He was staying at an hotel on the other side of the lake. Each day for the rest of the fortnight he rowed over to meet them at ten in the morning, sometimes spending the whole day with them. Trudy was charmed, she could hardly believe in Gwen's friendly indifference to him, notwithstanding he was a teacher at the same grammar school as Gwen, who therefore saw him every day.

Every time he met them he kissed Gwen on the cheek.

'You seem to be on very good terms with him,' Trudy said.

'Oh, Richard's an old friend. I've known him for years.'

The second week, Gwen went off on various expeditions of her own and left them together.

'This is quite a connoisseur's place,' Richard informed Trudy, and he pointed out why, and in what choice way, it was so, and Trudy, charmed, saw in the peeling pastel stucco of the little town, the unnecessary floral balconies, the bulbous Slovene spires, something special after all. She felt she saw, through his eyes, a precious rightness in the women with their grey skirts and well-filled blouses who trod beside their husbands and their clean children.

'Are they all Austrians?' Trudy asked.

'No, some of them are German and French. But this place attracts the same type.'

Richard's eyes rested with appreciation on the young noisy campers whose tents were pitched in the lake-side field. The campers were long-limbed and animal, brightly and briefly dressed. They romped like galvanized goats, yet looked surprisingly virtuous.

'What are they saying to each other?' she enquired of Richard when a group of them passed by, shouting some words and laughing at each other through glistening red lips and very white teeth.

'They are talking about their fast M.G. racing cars.'

'Oh, have they got racing cars?'

'No, the racing cars they are talking about don't exist. Sometimes they talk about their film contracts which don't exist. That's why they laugh.'

'Not much of a sense of humour, have they?'

'They are of mixed nationalities, so they have to limit their humour to jokes which everyone can understand, and so they talk about racing cars which aren't there.'

Trudy giggled a little, to show willing. Richard told her he was thirty-five, which she thought feasible. She volunteered that she was not quite twenty-two. Whereupon Richard looked at her and looked away, and looked again and took her hand. For, as he told Gwen afterwards, this remarkable statement was almost an invitation to a love affair.

Their love affair began that afternoon, in a boat on the

lake, when, barefoot, they had a game of placing sole to sole, heel to heel. Trudy squealed, and leaned back hard, pressing her feet against Richard's.

She squealed at Gwen when they met in their room later on. 'I'm having a heavenly time with Richard. I do so much like an older man.'

Gwen sat on her bed and gave Trudy a look of wonder. Then she said, 'He's not much older than you.'

'I've knocked a bit off my age,' Trudy said. 'Do you mind not letting on?'

'How much have you knocked off?'

'Seven years.'

'Very courageous,' Gwen said.

'What do you mean?'

'That you are brave.'

'Don't you think you're being a bit nasty?'

'No. It takes courage to start again and again. That's all I mean. Some women would find it boring.'

'Oh, I'm not an experienced girl at all,' Trudy said. 'Whatever made you think I was experienced?'

'It's true,' Gwen said, 'you show no signs of having profited by experience. Have you ever found it a successful tactic to remain twenty-two?'

'I believe you're jealous,' Trudy said. 'One expects this sort of thing from most older women, but somehow I didn't expect it from you.'

'One is always learning,' Gwen said.

Trudy fingered her curls. 'Yes, I have got a lot to learn from life,' she said, looking out of the window.

'God,' said Gwen, 'you haven't begun to believe that you're still twenty-two, have you?'

'Not quite twenty-two is how I put it to Richard.' Trudy said, 'and yes, I do feel it. That's my point. I don't feel a day older.'

*

The last day of their holidays Richard took Trudy rowing on the lake, which reflected a grey low sky.

'It looks like Windermere today, doesn't it?' he said.

Trudy had not seen Windermere, but she said, yes it did, and gazed at him with shining twenty-two-year-old eyes.

'Sometimes this place,' he said, 'is very like Yorkshire, but only when the weather's bad. Or, over on the mountain side, Wales.'

'Exactly what I told Gwen,' Trudy said. 'I said Wales, I said, it's like Wales.'

'Well, of course, there's quite a difference, really. It – '

'But Gwen simply squashed the idea. You see, she's an older woman, and being a schoolmistress – it's so much different when a man's a teacher – being a woman teacher, she feels she can treat me like a kid. I suppose I must expect it.'

'Oh well – '

'How long have you known Gwen?'

'Several years,' he said. 'Gwen's all right, darling. A great friend of my mother, is Gwen. Quite a member of the family.'

Trudy wanted to move her lodgings in London but she was prevented from doing so by a desire to be near Gwen, who saw Richard daily at school, and who knew his mother so well. And therefore Gwen's experience of Richard filled in the gaps in his life which were unknown to Trudy and which intrigued her.

She would fling herself into Gwen's room. Gwen, what d'you think? There he was waiting outside the office and he drove me home, and he's calling for me at seven, and next week-end . . .'

Gwen frequently replied, 'You are out of breath. Have you got heart trouble?' – for Gwen's room was only on the first floor. And Trudy was furious with Gwen on these occasions for seeming not to understand that the breathlessness was all part of her only being twenty-two, and excited by the boy-friend.

'I think Richard's so exciting,' Trudy said. 'It's difficult to believe I've only known him a month.'

'Has he invited you home to meet his mother?' Gwen enquired.

'No – not yet. Oh, do you think he will?'

'Yes, I think so. One day I'm sure he will.'

'Oh, do you mean it?' Trudy flung her arms girlishly round Gwen's impassive neck.

'When is your father coming up?' Gwen said.

'Not for ages, if at all. He can't leave Leicester just now, and he hates London.'

'You must get him to come and ask Richard what his intentions are. A young girl like you needs protection.'

'Gwen, don't be silly.'

Often Trudy would question Gwen about Richard and his mother.

'Are they well off? Is she a well-bred woman? What's the house like? How long have you known Richard? Why hasn't he married before? The mother, is she – '

'Lucy is a marvel in her way,' Gwen said.

'Oh, do you call her Lucy? You must know her awfully well.'

'I'm quite,' said Gwen, 'a member of the family in my way.'

'Richard has often told me that. Do you go there *every* Sunday?'

'Most Sundays,' Gwen said. 'It is often very amusing, and one sometimes sees a fresh face.'

'Why,' Trudy said, as the summer passed and she had already been away for several week-ends with Richard, 'doesn't he ask me to meet his mother? If my mother were alive and living in London I know I would have asked him home to meet her.'

Trudy threw out hints to Richard. 'How I wish you could meet my father. You simply must come up to Leicester in the Christmas holidays and stay with him. He's rather tied up in Leicester and never leaves it. He's an insurance manager. The successful kind.'

'I can't very well leave Mother at Christmas,' Richard said, 'but I'd love to meet your father some other time.' His tan had worn off, and Trudy thought him more distinguished and at the same time more unattainable than ever.

'I think it only right,' Trudy said in her young young way, 'that one should introduce the man one loves to one's parents' – for it was agreed between them that they were in love.

But still, by the end of October, Richard had not asked her to meet his mother.

'Does it matter all that much?' Gwen said.

'Well, it would be a definite step forward,' Trudy said. 'We can't go on being just friends like this. I'd like to know where I stand with him. After all, we're in love and we're both free. Do you know, I'm beginning to think he hasn't any serious intentions after all. But if he asked me to meet his mother it would be a sort of sign, wouldn't it?'

'It certainly would,' Gwen said.

'I don't even feel I can ring him up at home until I've met his mother. I'd feel shy of talking to her on the phone. I must meet her. It's becoming a sort of obsession.'

'It certainly is,' Gwen said. 'Why don't you just say to him, "I'd like to meet your mother"?'

'Well, Gwen, there are some things a girl can't say.'

'No, but a woman can.'

'Are you going on about my age again? I tell you, Gwen, I feel twenty-two. I think twenty-two. I am twenty-two so far as Richard's concerned. I don't think really you can help me much. After all, you haven't been successful with men yourself, have you?'

'No,' Gwen said, 'I haven't. I've always been on the old side.'

'That's just my point. It doesn't get you anywhere to feel old and think old. If you want to be successful with men you have to hang on to your youth.'

'It wouldn't be worth it at the price,' Gwen said, 'to judge by the state you're in.'

Trudy started to cry and ran to her room, presently returning to ask Gwen questions about Richard's mother. She could rarely keep away from Gwen when she was not out with Richard.

'What's his mother really like? Do you think I'd get on with her?'

'If you wish I'll take you to see his mother one Sunday.'

'No, no,' Trudy said. 'It's got to come from him if it has any meaning. The invitation must come from Richard.'

Trudy had almost lost her confidence, and in fact had come to wonder if Richard was getting tired of her, since he had less and less time to spare for her, when unexpectedly and yet so inevitably, in November, he said, 'You must come and meet my mother.'

'Oh!' Trudy said.

'I should like you to meet my mother. She's looking forward to it.'

'Oh, does she know about me?'

'Rather.'

'Oh!'

'It's happened. Everything's all right,' Trudy said breathlessly.

'He has asked you home to meet his mother,' Gwen said

135

without looking up from the exercise book she was correcting.

'It's important to me, Gwen.'

'Yes, yes,' Gwen said.

'I'm going on Sunday afternoon,' Trudy said. 'Will you be there?'

'Not till supper time,' Gwen said. 'Don't worry.'

'He said, "I want you to meet Mother. I've told her all about you."'

'All about you?'

'That's what he said, and it means so much to me, Gwen. So much.'

Gwen said, 'It's a beginning.'

'Oh, it's the beginning of everything. I'm sure of that.'

Richard picked her up in his Singer at four on Sunday. He seemed preoccupied. He did not, as usual, open the car door for her, but slid into the driver's seat and waited for her to get in beside him. She fancied he was perhaps nervous about her meeting his mother for the first time.

The house on Campion Hill was delightful. They must be very *comfortable*, Trudy thought. Mrs Seeton was a tall, stooping woman, well dressed and preserved, with thick steel-grey hair and large light eyes. 'I hope you'll call me Lucy,' she said. 'Do you smoke?'

'I don't,' said Trudy.

'Helps the nerves,' said Mrs Seeton, 'when one is getting on in life. You don't need to smoke yet awhile.'

'No,' Trudy said. 'What a lovely room, Mrs Seeton.'

'*Lucy*,' said Mrs Seeton.

'Lucy,' Trudy said, very shyly, and looked at Richard for support. But he was drinking the last of his tea and looking out of the window as if to see whether the sky had cleared.

'Richard has to go out for supper,' Mrs Seeton said, waving her cigarette holder very prettily. 'Don't forget to watch the time, Richard. But Trudy will stay to supper with

136

me, I *hope*. Trudy and I have a lot to talk about, I'm sure.'
She looked at Trudy and very faintly, with no more than a
butterfly-flick, winked.

Trudy accepted the invitation with a conspiratorial nod
and a slight squirm in her chair. She looked at Richard to
see if he would say where he was going for supper, but he
was gazing up at the top pane of the window, his fingers
tapping on the arm of the shining Old Windsor chair on
which he sat.

Richard left at half-past six, very much more cheerful in
his going than he had been in his coming.

'Richard gets restless on a Sunday,' said his mother.

'Yes, so I've noticed,' Trudy said, so that there should be
no mistake about who had been occupying his recent
Sundays.

'I dare say now you want to hear all about Richard,' said
his mother in a secretive whisper, although no one was in
earshot. Mrs Seeton giggled through her nose and raised
her shoulders all the way up her long neck till they almost
touched her ear-rings.

Trudy vaguely copied her gesture. 'Oh yes,' she said,
'Mrs Seeton.'

'Lucy. You must call me Lucy, now, you know. I want
you and me to be friends. I want you to feel like a member
of the family. Would you like to see the house?'

She led the way upstairs and displayed her affluent
bedroom, one wall of which was entirely covered by mirror,
so that, for every photograph on her dressing-table of
Richard and Richard's late father, there were virtually two
photographs in the room.

'This is Richard on his pony, Lob. He adored Lob. We all
adored Lob. Of course, we were in the country then. This is
Richard with Nana. And this is Richard's father at the
outbreak of war. What did you do in the war, dear?'

'I was at school,' Trudy said, quite truthfully.

'Oh, then you're a teacher, too?'

'No, I'm a secretary. I didn't leave school till after the war.'

Mrs Seeton said, looking at Trudy from two angles, 'Good gracious me, how deceiving. I thought you were about Richard's age, like Gwen. Gwen is such a dear. This is Richard as a graduate. Why he went into schoolmastering I don't know. Still, he's a very good master. Gwen always says so, quite definitely. Don't you adore Gwen?'

'Gwen is a good bit older than me,' Trudy said, being still upset on the subject of age.

'She ought to be here any moment. She usually comes for supper. Now I'll show you the other rooms and Richard's room.'

When they came to Richard's room his mother stood on the threshold and, with her finger to her lips for no apparent reason, swung the door open. Compared with the rest of the house this was a bleak, untidy, almost schoolboy's room. Richard's green pyjama trousers lay on the floor where he had stepped out of them. This was a sight familiar to Trudy from her several week-end excursions with Richard, of late months, to hotels up the Thames valley.

'So untidy,' said Richard's mother, shaking her head woefully. 'So untidy. One day, Trudy, dear, we must have a real chat.'

Gwen arrived presently, and made herself plainly at home by going straight into the kitchen to prepare a salad. Mrs Seeton carved slices of cold meat while Trudy stood and watched them both, listening to a conversation between them which indicated a long intimacy. Richard's mother seemed anxious to please Gwen.

'Expecting Grace tonight?' Gwen said.

'No, darling, I thought perhaps not *tonight*. Was I right?'

'Oh, of course, yes. Expecting Joanna?'

'Well, as it's Trudy's *first* visit, I thought perhaps not – '

138

'Would you,' Gwen said to Trudy, 'lay the table, my dear. Here are the knives and forks.'

Trudy bore these knives and forks into the dining-room with a sense of having been got rid of with a view to being talked about.

At supper, Mrs Seeton said, 'It seems a bit odd, there only being the three of us. We usually have such jolly Sunday suppers. Next week, Trudy, you must come and meet the whole crowd – mustn't she, Gwen?'

'Oh yes,' Gwen said, 'Trudy must do that.'

Towards half-past ten Richard's mother said, 'I doubt if Richard will be back in time to run you home. Naughty boy, I daren't think what he gets up to.'

On the way to the bus stop Gwen said, 'Are you happy now that you've met Lucy?'

'Yes, I think so. But I think Richard might have stayed. It would have been nice. I dare say he wanted me to get to know his mother by myself. But in fact I felt the need of his support.'

'Didn't you have a talk with Lucy?'

'Well yes, but not much really. Richard probably didn't realize you were coming to supper. Richard probably thought his mother and I could have a heart-to-heart – '

'I usually go to Lucy's on Sunday,' Gwen said.

'Why?'

'Well, she's a friend of mine. I know her ways. She amuses me.'

During the week Trudy saw Richard only once, for a quick drink.

'Exams,' he said. 'I'm rather busy, darling.'

'Exams in November? I thought they started in December.'

'Preparation for exams,' he said. 'Preliminaries. Lots of work.' He took her home, kissed her on the cheek and drove off.

She looked after the car, and for a moment hated his moustache. But she pulled herself together and, recalling her youthfulness, decided she was too young really to judge the fine shades and moods of a man like Richard.

He picked her up at four o'clock on Sunday.

'Mother's looking forward to seeing you,' he said. 'She hopes you will stay for supper.'

'You won't have to go out, will you, Richard?'

'Not tonight, no.'

But he did have to go out to keep an appointment of which his mother reminded him immediately after tea. He had smiled at his mother and said, 'Thanks.'

Trudy saw the photograph album, then she heard how Mrs Seeton had met Richard's father in Switzerland, and what Mrs Seeton had been wearing at the time.

At half-past six the supper party arrived. These were three women, including Gwen. The one called Grace was quite pretty, with a bewildered air. The one called Iris was well over forty and rather loud in her manner.

'Where's Richard tonight, the old cad?' said Iris.

'How do I know?' said his mother. 'Who am I to ask?'

'Well, at least he's a hard worker during the week. A brilliant teacher,' said doe-eyed Grace.

'Middling as a schoolmaster,' Gwen said.

'Oh, Gwen! Look how long he's held down the job,' his mother said.

'I should think,' Grace said, 'he's wonderful with the boys.'

'Those Shakespearean productions at the end of the summer term are really magnificent,' Iris bawled. 'I'll hand him that, the old devil.'

'Magnificent,' said his mother. 'You must admit, Gwen – '

'Very middling performances,' Gwen said.

'I suppose you are right, but, after all, they are only

140

schoolboys. You can't do much with untrained actors, Gwen,' said Mrs Seeton very sadly.

'I adore Richard,' Iris said, 'when he's in his busy, occupied mood. He's so – '

'Oh yes,' Grace said, 'Richard is wonderful when he's got a lot on his mind.'

'I know,' said his mother. 'There was one time when Richard had just started teaching – I must tell you this story – he . . .'

Before they left Mrs Seeton said to Trudy, 'You will come with Gwen next week, won't you? I want you to regard yourself as one of us. There are two other friends of Richard's I do want you to meet. Old friends.'

On the way to the bus Trudy said to Gwen, 'Don't you find it dull going to Mrs Seeton's every Sunday?'

'Well, yes, my dear young thing, and no. From time to time one sees a fresh face, and then it's quite amusing.'

'Doesn't Richard ever stay at home on a Sunday evening?'

'No, I can't say he does. In fact, he's very often away for the whole week-end. As you know.'

'Who are these women?' Trudy said, stopping in the street.

'Oh, just old friends of Richard's.'

'Do they see him often?'

'Not now. They've become members of the family.'

Alice Long's Dachshunds

The guns clank on the stone, one after the other, echoing against the walls outside the chapel, as the men come in for Mass before the shoot. Mamie, whose age is eight years and two months, kneels in the second row from the back, on the right-hand side, near the Virgin, where a warm candle is lit. There is no other warmth. Alice Long is kneeling on a front hassock. Her two brothers from London have come in – tall men in knickerbockers and green wool stockings that stride past Mamie's eyes as she kneels in her place.

Other big men have put their guns against the wall outside the chapel door. The Catholics from the cottages have come in. Everyone except the strangers is praying for more snow and a road blockage to the town, so that poor Alice Long can decently serve roe deer, roe deer, roe deer for all the meals that the London people are going to eat. The woods are cracking alive with roe deer, but meat from the town has got to be paid for with money.

Alice Long is round-shouldered and worried; she is the only daughter of old Sir Martin, and is always addressed, to her face, as Miss Long. Her money is her own, but it goes into the keeping of the House.

Alice Long's two brothers' wives have come into the chapel now. They are the last, because they have to look after their own babies when they get up. Before Mamie's birth, all the babies in the house had nurses. The two wives were differently made from the start, before they became Alice Long's sisters-in-law, and still look so, although their tweed coats were made more alike. One is called Lady Caroline and the other, Mrs Martin Long, will be Lady

Long when old Sir Martin dies and Martin Long comes into the title.

Mamie is watching Lady Caroline through her fingers. Lady Caroline is big and broad, with bobbed black hair under her black lace veil; she doesn't like Alice Long's dogs, and dogs are the only things Alice Long has for herself. Alice Long was made to be kept down by upkeep.

The big clock upstairs chimes seven. The priest comes in and the feet shuffle. Mamie cannot see the altar when everyone is standing. She stares at the candle. The service begins. Will the friends who have come from warm London catch their death of colds?

Mamie stops in the snow. The ends of the dogs' leashes are wound round her hands in their woollen gloves, three round the right hand and two round the left. She unwinds the leads to give her arms scope, and the dogs take advantage of the few extra inches of freedom, snuffling and wriggling away from Mamie until the leads pull taut. But she works them back, lifting her elbows to cup her hands to her mouth.

'Come out. I can see you.'

No reply.

She repeats the words and drops her arms, aching from the weight of straining dogs.

There is a thud of snowfall from the clump of trees. The noise would have been only a little plop had there been any more sound besides that of the snuffling dogs.

She is taking Alice Long's dogs for a walk.

'She'll be glad to, Miss Long,' said her mother. 'Tomorrow after school. It's a half day.'

This morning, her mother said, 'Come straight home at two for Alice Long's dogs.'

To do so, Mamie has missed her dancing lesson at the convent. She is learning the sword dance. Alice Long had got her into the convent at reduced fees, and even those reduced fees Alice Long pays herself. She likes to keep the Catholic tenants Catholic.

Mamie walks on, satisfied there are no boys behind the trees. She is afraid the boys will find her and tease the dogs, laugh at her, laugh at the little padding, waddling dogs, do them harm before they can be returned to the House.

The snow in the wood is too deep for low-made dogs. Mamie wanders around the edge of the wood, on the crunchy path, with little running steps every now and then as the dogs get the better of her.

'My dachshunds,' said Alice Long lovingly.

The country people said to each other, when she was out of sight, 'Alice Long has only got her dogs. And all that upkeep.'

'Lady Caroline hates dogs.'

'No, she only hates dachshunds. German sausages. She likes big dogs for the country.'

Alice Long is sitting with her teacup in Mamie's house, which has five rooms plus k.p.b. – standing for kitchen, pantry, and bathroom – and is semi-detached. Next door are Alice Long's Couple. Mamie's father no longer works on the estate but is a foreman in the town at Heppleford and Styles' Linoleum.

'Lady Caroline can't bear them. They've been locked in the north wing since Friday. I have to keep a fire going . . .'

'That wing's not heated, of course.'

'No. They are freezing and lonely. I keep putting logs on. I get up in the middle of the night to see to the fire.'

'They'll be all right, Miss Long.'

'They need a good run, that's all. I won't have time for the dogs today. But the family goes home tomorrow or Wednesday . . .'

Mamie has taken the dogs out for a run before. She is not allowed to go near the wood but must keep to the inhabited paths that pass the groups of houses on the estate and lead to the shop. Near the shop are usually the children from the village school, throwing snowballs in winter, wheeling bicycles in summer. Mamie has money for toffee and an orange drink. She wanders by the wood.

Her father has been at home for three working days. There is a strike. Alice Long sits downstairs. The father has gone to wait upstairs until she leaves. Then he opens the cupboard door where the television set is placed in a recess formed by the removal of one of the shelves. Alice Long has not seen this television set. The people next door, her Couple, took on a television many years ago, and keep it out in the living room.

Mitzi, Fritzi, Blitzi, Ritzi, and Kitzy.

'Alice Long's dogs are all she's got to herself.'

The dogs go about together and sometimes all answer at once when Alice Long calls one of their names. Mamie does not know them apart. They vary slightly in size, fatness, and in the black scars on their brown coats.

The path has become a ridge of frozen earth where the field has been plowed right up to the verge of the wood. The daylight is turning blue with cold while Mamie struggles with the leads. One gumboot digs deep in a furrow and the other stabs to keep its hold on the ridge. The dogs snuffle each other and snort steam. They strain toward the wood, and Hamilton is suddenly there – Alice Long's game-keeper – coming out of the trees, tall and broad, with his grey moustache and deep-pink face. He looks at Mamie as if to say, 'Come here.' The dogs fuss round him, cutting into her gloves.

Mamie says, 'I've got to go that way,' pointing down toward her home across the field.

'I'll see you back at the House,' he says, and stoops back into the wood, examining the undergrown branches.

Hamilton looks after old Sir Martin when he becomes beyond a woman's strength.

'I'm afraid my father is not very well any more.'

'I don't know how you do it, Miss Long.'

145

Mamie's mother says that anybody else but Alice Long would have put the old man away.

Hamilton sees to the boilers that heat the heated wing. He has too much to do to air the dogs regularly.

'Without Hamilton, I don't know what we should do. Before your husband left us, we had it easier.'

Mamie has turned away from the wood. She has taken the path to the houses, looking back all the time to see whether Hamilton is following her with his eyes, those eyes that are two poached eggs grown old, looking at her every time he sees her.

She takes the footpath on the main road. The dogs are trotting now. A car passes, and a delivery van from the grocer's shop in the town. She clutches the leads.

'Don't let one of them get run over. Alice Long would be up to ninety-nine.'

She presses, at the sharp bend, into the high white bank which touches again on the wood, while a very big lorry carrying sacks of coal, creeps fearfully around as if bewaring of the dogs.

Bump on her shoulder, then bump on her cap come the snowballs. The boys are up there on the bank. She turns and looks quickly and sees parts of children ducking out of sight with short, laughing squeals. There are two girls with the boys; she has seen their hair. One of the girls wears the dark-blue convent cap.

'Connie, come down!'

'It isn't Connie,' Gwen's voice answers.

Gwen should be at the dancing class. She is learning to do the sword dance with Mamie.

A snowball falls on the road and bursts open. There is no stone inside it. The dogs are yelping now, pelted with snowballs. They are up to ninety-nine, not used to this.

Mamie drags them round the corner and starts to run. The children scramble down after her and catch up. She recognizes them all. She tries to gather up some snow, but it is impossible to make and throw a ball with the leads around her gloves.

'Where are you going with those dogs?' says a boy.

'To the shop, then up to the House.'

'They look dirty.'

Gwen says, 'Do you like those dogs?'

'Not all of them together.'

'Let them run loose,' says the other girl. 'It's good for them.'

'No.'

'Come on and play.'

She is scrambling up the bank, while everyone is trying to pull the dogs up by their leads or push them up by their bottoms.

'Lift them up. You'll throttle them!'

'Let go the leads. We'll take one each.'

'No.'

Up on the bank, Mamie says, 'I'll tie them to that tree.' She refuses to let the leads out of her own hands, but she permits two of the boys to make the knots secure, as they have learned to do in the Scout Cubs.

Then it is boys against girls in a snow fight, with such fast pelting and splutters from drenched faces, such loud shrieks that the dogs' coughing and whining can scarcely be heard. When it is time to go, Mamie counts the dogs. Then she starts to untie them. The knots are difficult. She calls after one of the boys to come and untie the knots, but he does not look around. Gwen returns; she stands and looks. Mamie is kneeling in the slush, trying.

'How do you untie these knots?' All the leads are mixed up in a knotted muddle.

'I don't know. What's their names?'

'Mitzi, Fritzi, Blitzi, Ritzi, and Kitzy.'

'Do you know one from the other?'

'No.'

Mamie bends down with her strong teeth in the leather. She has loosened the first knot. All the knots are coming loose. She gets her woollen gloves on again and starts to wind the leads around her hands. One of them springs from her grasp, and the little dog scuttles away into the wood among the old wet leaves, so that it seems to slither like a snake on its belly with its cord bouncing behind it.

'Mitzi! Kitzy! Blitzi!'

The dog disappears and the four in hand are excited, anxious to be free and warmed up, too.

'Catch him, Gwen! Can you see him? Where is it? Mitzi-mitzi-mitzi! Blitzi-blitzi!'

'I've got to go home,' Gwen says. 'You shouldn't have stopped to play.'

Gwen is Sister Monica's model pupil for punctuality, neatness, and truthfulness. Mamie has no ground to answer Gwen's reproach as the girl starts to clamber down the bank.

The wood is dark and there is no sound of the dog. Mamie squelches with the four dogs among the leaves and snow lumps. 'Fritzi-fritzi-fritzi mitzi!' A bark, a yap, behind her. Again a yap-yap. She turns and finds the dog tied once more to a tree. Hamilton? She peers all around her and sees nobody.

She should be hurrying toward the drive, but she is too tired to hurry. The Lodge gates are still open, although the sky looks late. The lights are on in the Lodge, which has been let to new people from Liverpool for their week-ends. They are having a long week-end this time. A young woman comes out to her car as Mamie comes in the gateway with the five dogs.

'Goodness, you're wet through!'

'I got in a snowdrift.'

'Hurry home then, dear, and get changed.'

Mamie cannot hurry. She is not very well any more, like old Sir Martin. She is not very real any more. The colour of the afternoon seems strange and the sky is banked with snowdrifts. She runs in little spurts only in obedience to the pull of the dogs. But she draws them as tight as she can and plods in the direction of the House. She turns to the right when she reaches the wide steps and the big front doors. Around to the right and into the yard, where Hamilton's door is. She tries to open his door. It is locked. To pull the bell would require raising her arm, and she is too tired to do so. She tries to knock. The dogs are full of noise and anxiety, are scratching the door to get inside. She looks at them and with difficulty switches those leads in her right hand to her left, winding them round her wrist, since the hand is already full. While she knocks with her free hand at the door, she realizes that she has noticed something. There are only four dogs now. She counts – one, two, three, four. She counts the leads – one, two, three, four. She looks away again and knocks. It has not happened. Nothing has happened. It is not real. She knocks again. Hamilton is coming.

'Their food's in there,' Hamilton says, not looking at the dogs but opening the door that leads from his room to another, more cluttered room. He lets the dogs scuttle in to their food without counting them. He does not remove their leads but throws them onto the floor to trail behind them. Finally, he shuts the inner door on them. He sits down in his chair and looks at Mamie as if to say, 'Come here.'

'I've got to go home.'

'You're wet through. Get dry by the fire a minute. I'll get you a lift home.'

'No, I'm late.'

He pats his knee. 'Sit here, dearie, lass.' He has a glass and a bottle by him. 'I want to give you a drop. Come on. I don't want sex.'

She perches on his lap. He has not counted the dogs. Alice Long will be up to ninety-nine, but it's Hamilton's fault from now. Hamilton has taken the dogs.

'Now sip.'

She recognizes whisky.

'Take a good swallow.'

He gives her a lemon drop to hide her breath, then gives her a kiss on her mouth while she is still sucking the sweet.

'I'm going now. I hope the dogs are all right.'

'Oh, the dogs, they're all right.'

He takes her hand and goes to find one of the workmen who are mending the House. Alice Long is not home yet from her meeting, and she will not miss the workman for a few minutes.

Mamie climbs into the foreman's car beside the workman. The seat is covered with white dust, but she does not brush it off the seat before sliding onto it. Her clothes will be spoiled. She feels safe beside the driver. The whisky has given her back a real afternoon.

'What's the time, please?' she asks.

'About twenty past four.'

The man backs and turns. Hamilton has gone into his quarters. The car skirts the House, turning by the large new clearing where, in the summer, the tourists' coaches come.

'You can't get many up here in Northumberland. They all swarm to the old houses in the South. Here, it's out of the way . . .'

'Well, it's an experience for those who do come, Miss Long. Especially the Catholics.'

The House was once turned into a hospital for the wounded English soldiers after the Battle of Flodden, which the English won.

The House was a Mass centre at the times of the Catholic Persecution. Outside the armoury, there is a chalice in a glass case dating from Elizabethan times. It has been sold to a museum, but the museum allows the family to keep it at the House during Sir Martin's lifetime. Mamie has been inside the priest hole, where the priests were hidden when the House was searched for priests; they would sometimes stay there several days. The hole is a large space behind a panel that comes out of the wall, up among the attics. You can stand in the priest hole and look up at the beams, where, in those days, food was always stored in case of emergency.

The workmen are mending the roof.

'Did you see the priest hole?' Mamie feels talkative.

'What's that?'

'A place where the priests used to hide, up in the roof. It's historic. Haven't you seen it?'

'No, but I seen plenty dry rot up there in that roof.'

The gates are closed. The man gets out to open them; then he drives off again.

Is it possible that one of the dogs is lost? Mamie is confused. There must have been five. I found the lost one, tied to the tree. But then she sees herself again counting them outside Hamilton's door. One, two, three, four. Only four. No, no, no, it's not real. Hamilton has taken the dogs. It's for him to count.

The workman says, 'Do you like the Beatles?'

'Oh, yes, they're great. Do you like them?'

'So-so. I'd like just one day's earnings that the Beatles get. Just one day. I could retire on it.'

Sister Monica has said that there is no harm in the Beatles, and then Mamie felt indignant because it showed Sister Monica did not properly appreciate them. She ought to lump them together with things like whisky, smoking, and sex; the Beatles are quite good enough to be forbidden.

'I like dancing,' Mamie says.

'Rock-'n-roll stuff?'

'Yes, but at school we only get folk dancing. I'm learning the sword dance. It's historic in the Border country.'

151

All the rest of the week, she hurries home from school to see if Alice Long has been to see her mother about the missing dog.

I counted. One, two, three, four. But I had five when I left the wood. I brought five out of the wood, and up the hill. I had five at the Lodge. I must have had . . .

Alice Long will be up to ninety-nine. She will come to Mamie's house to make inquiries:

'Hamilton says she only brought four . . .

'Hamilton says he didn't count them, he just took the leads from her hand . . .

'Hamilton must have been drinking and let one of them slip out of the door . . .

'I've only just counted them. One must have been missing since Monday. When Mamie . . .'

By Friday, Alice Long has not come. Mamie's mother says, 'Alice Long hasn't dropped in. I must take a pie up to the House on Monday and see what's doing.'

On Sunday afternoon, Alice Long's car stops at the door. 'Come in, Miss Long, come in. Have you no family down this weekend?'

Mamie's father shuts away the television, puts on his coat, says good afternoon, and goes upstairs.

Alice Long sits trembling on the sofa beside Mamie while her mother puts on the tea.

She says, 'It's Hamilton.'

'The same thing again?'

'No, worse. A tragedy.' Alice Long shuts her lips tight and pats Mamie's hair. Her hand is shaking.

'Mamie, go out and play,' says her mother.

When Alice Long has driven her car away, Mamie comes in with the ends of her skipping-rope twined around her gloves. Her father comes down, takes off his coat, and opens up the television. 'Oh, don't turn it on,' says her mother, in anguish.

Mamie eats some of the remnants of cake and sandwiches while she listens.

'Hanging in the priest hole – all of them. She looked for them all night. Hamilton's gone, cleared off. It's the drink. The police have got a warrant out. They were found hanged on the beams after Mass this morning. Didn't I say poor Alice Long was looking bad at Mass? I thought it must be her father again. But she'd been up all night looking for the dogs, and at Mass she still didn't know where they were. It was after Mass they found them, herself and Mrs Huddlestone. Think of the sight! Five of them hanging in a row. Poor little beasts. Hamilton disappeared yesterday. They'll get him, though, just wait.'

'He's a bit of a lunatic,' Mamie's father says.

'Lunatic! He's vicious. He ought to be hung himself. They were all Alice Long had. But he'll be caught!'

Her father says, 'I doubt it. Not Hamilton. Even the roe-buck called him Pussyfoot.' He laughs at his own joke. The mother turns away her head.

Mamie says, 'How many were hanging in the priest hole?'

'All of them in a row.'

'How many?'

'Five. You know she had five. You took them out, didn't you?'

Mamie says, 'I was only wondering if there was *room* for five in the priest hole. Did she really say there were five? It wasn't four?'

'She said all five of them. What are you talking about, no room in the priest hole? There's plenty room. He'd have killed six if she'd had six. She was so good to him.'

'A shocking affair,' says her father.

Mamie feels weightless as daylight. She waves her arms as if they are freed of a huge harness.

'Five of them.' I counted wrong. I didn't lose one. There were five.

153

She skips over to fetch the shining brass pokers from the fender and places them crisscross on the linoleum to practise her sword dance. Then she starts to dance, heel-and-toe, heel-and-toe, over-and-across, one-two-three, one-two-three. Her mother stands amazed and is about to say stop it at once, this is no time to practise, children have no heart, Alice Long pays your school fees and I thought you loved animals. But her father is clapping his hands in time to her dancing – one-two-three, heel-and-toe, hand-on-hip, right-hand, left-hand, cross-and-back. Then her father starts to sing as well, loudly, tara rum-tum-tum, tara rum-tum-tum, clapping his hands while she dances the jig, and there isn't a thing anyone can do about it.

The Fathers' Daughters

She left the old man in his deck-chair on the front, having first adjusted the umbrella awning with her own hand, and with her own hand, put his panama hat at a comfortable angle. The beach attendant had been sulky, but she didn't see why one should lay out tips only for adjusting an umbrella and a panama hat. Since the introduction of the new franc it was impossible to tip less than a franc. There seemed to be a conspiracy all along the coast to hide the lesser coins from the visitors, and one could only find franc pieces in one's purse, and one had to be careful not to embarrass Father, and one . . .

She hurried along the Rue Paradis, keeping in the hot shade, among all the old, old smells of Nice, not only garlic wafting from the cafés, and of the hot invisible air itself, but the smells from her memory, from thirty-five summers at Nice in apartments of long ago, Father's summer salon, Father's friends' children, Father's friends, writers, young artists dating back five years at Nice, six, nine years; and then, before the war, twenty years ago – when we were at Nice, do you remember, Father? Do you remember the pension on the Boulevard Victor Hugo when we were rather poor? Do you remember the Americans at the Negresco in 1937 – how changed, how demure they are now! Do you remember, Father, how in the old days we disliked the thick carpets – at least, you disliked them, and what you dislike, I dislike, isn't it so, Father?

Yes, Dora, we don't care for luxury. Comfort, yes, but luxury, no.

I doubt if we can afford to stay at an hotel on the front this year, Father.

What's that? What's that you say?

I said I doubt if we ought to stay on the front this year, Father; the Promenade des Anglais is becoming very trippery. Remember you disliked the thick carpets . . .

Yes, yes, of course.

Of course, and so we'll go, I suggest, to a little place I've found on the Boulevard Gambetta, and if we don't like that there's a very good place on the Boulevard Victor Hugo. Within our means, Father, modest and . . .

What's that you say?

I said it wasn't a vulgar place, Father.

Ah. No.

And so I'll just drop them a note and book a couple of bedrooms. They may be small, but the food . . .

Facing the sea, Dora.

They are all very vulgar places facing the sea, Father. Very distracting. No peace at all. Times have changed, you know.

Ah. Well, I leave it to you, dear. Tell them I desire a large room, suitable for entertaining. Spare no expense, Dora.

Oh, of course not, Father.

And I hope to God we've won the lottery, she thought, as she hurried up the little street to the lottery kiosk. Someone's got to win it out of the whole of France. The dark-skinned blonde at the lottery kiosk took an interest in Dora, who came so regularly each morning rather than buy a newspaper to see the results. She leaned over the ticket, holding her card of numbers, comparing it with Dora's ticket, with an expression of earnest sympathy.

'No luck,' Dora said.

'Try again tomorrow,' said the woman. 'One never knows. Life is a lottery . . .'

Dora smiled as one who must either smile or weep. On her way back to the sea front she thought, tomorrow I will buy five hundred francs' worth. Then she thought, no, no, I'd better not, I may run short of francs and have to take Father home before time. Dora, the food here is inferior. – I know, Father, but it's the same everywhere in France now, times have changed. – I think we should move to another hotel, Dora. – The others are all very expensive, Father. – What's that? What's that you say? – There are no other rooms available, Father, because of the tourists, these days.

The brown legs of lovely young men and girls passed her as she approached the sea. I ought to appreciate every minute of this, she thought, it may be the last time. This thoroughly blue sea, these brown limbs, these white teeth and innocent inane tongues, these palm trees – all this is what we are paying for.

'Everything all right, Father?'

'Where have you been, dear?'

'Only for a walk round the back streets to smell the savours.'

'Dora, you are a chip off the old block. What did you see?'

'Brown limbs, white teeth, men in shirt sleeves behind café windows, playing cards with green bottles in front of them.'

'Good – you see everything with my eyes, Dora.'

'Heat, smell, brown legs – it's what we are paying for, Father.'

'Dora, you are becoming vulgar, if you don't mind my saying so. The eye of the true artist doesn't see life in the way of goods paid for. The world is ours. It is our birthright. We take it without payment.'

'I'm not an artist like you, Father. Let me move the umbrella – you mustn't get too much sun.'

'Times have changed,' he said, glancing along the pebble beach, 'the young men today have no interest in life.'

She knew what her father meant. All along the beach, the young men playing with the air, girls, the sun; they were coming in from the sea, shaking the water from their heads; they were walking over the pebbles, then splashing into the water; they were taking an interest in their environment with every pore of their skin, as Father would have said in younger days when he was writing his books. What he meant, now, when he said, 'the young men today have no interest in life' was that his young disciples, his admirers, had all gone, they were grown old and preoccupied, and had not been replaced. The last young man to seek out Father had been a bloodless-looking youth – not that one judged by appearances – who had called about seven years ago at their house in Essex. Father had made the most of him, giving up many of his mornings to sitting in the library talking about books with the young man, about life and the old days. But this, the last of Father's disciples, had left after two weeks with a promise to send them the article he was going to write about Father and his works. Indeed he had sent a letter: 'Dear Henry Castlemaine, – Words cannot express my admiration . . .' After that they had heard no more. Dora was not really sorry. He was a poor specimen compared with the men who, in earlier days, used to visit Father. Dora in her late teens could have married one of three or four vigorous members of the Henry Castlemaine set, but she had not done so because of her widowed father and his needs as a public figure; and now she sometimes felt it would have served Father better if she had married, because of Father – one could have contributed from a husband's income, perhaps, to his declining years.

Dora said, 'We must be going back to the hotel for lunch.'

'Let us lunch somewhere else. The food there is . . .'

She helped her father from the deck-chair and, turning to

158

the sea, took a grateful breath of the warm blue breeze. A young man, coming up from the sea, shook his head blindly and splashed her with water; then noticing what he had done he said – turning and catching her by the arm – 'Oh, I'm so sorry.' He spoke in English, was an Englishman, and she knew already how unmistakably she was an English-woman. 'All right,' she said, with a quick little laugh. The father was fumbling with his stick, the incident had passed, was immediately forgotten by Dora as she took his arm and propelled him across the wide hot boulevard where the white-suited policemen held up the impetuous traffic. 'How would you like to be arrested by one of those, Dora?' He gave his deep short laugh and looked down at her. 'I'd love it, Father.' Perhaps he wouldn't insist on lunching else-where. If only they could reach the hotel, it would be all right; Father would be too exhausted to insist. But already he was saying, 'Let's find somewhere for lunch.'

'Well, we've paid for it at the hotel, Father.'

'Don't be vulgar, my love.'

In the following March, when Dora met Ben Donadieu for the first time, she had the feeling she had seen him somewhere before, she knew not where. Later, she told him of this, but he could not recall having seen her. But this sense of having seen him somewhere remained with Dora all her life. She came to believe she had met him in a former existence. In fact, it was on the beach at Nice that she had seen him, when he came up among the pebbles from the sea, and shook his hair, wetting her, and took her arm, apologizing.

'Don't be vulgar, my love. The hotel food is appalling. Not French at all.'

'It's the same all over France, Father, these days.'

'There used to be a restaurant – what was its name? – in one of those little streets behind the Casino. Let's go there. All the writers go there.'

'Not any more, Father.'

'Well, so much the better. Let's go there in any case. What's the name of the place? – Anyway, come on, I could go there blindfold. All the writers used to go . . .'

She laughed, because, after all, he was sweet. As she walked with him towards the Casino she did not say – Not any more, Father, do the writers go there. The writers don't come to Nice, not those of moderate means. But there's one writer here this year, Father, called Kenneth Hope, whom you haven't heard about. He uses our beach, and I've seen him once – a shy, thin, middle-aged man. But he won't speak to anyone. He writes wonderfully, Father. I've read his novels, they open windows in the mind that have been bricked-up for a hundred years. I have read *The Inventors*, which made great fame and fortune for him. It is about the inventors of patent gadgets, what lives they lead, how their minds apply themselves to invention and to love, and you would think, while you were reading *The Inventors*, that the place they live in was dominated by inventors. He has that magic, Father – he can make you believe anything. Dora did not say this, for her father had done great work too, and deserved a revival. His name was revered, his books were not greatly spoken of, they were not read. He would not understand the fame of Kenneth Hope. Father's novels were about the individual consciences of men and women, no one could do the individual conscience like Father. 'Here we are, Father – this is the place, isn't it?'

'No, Dora, it's further along.'

'Oh, but that's the Tumbril; it's wildly expensive.'

'Really, darling!'

She decided to plead the heat, and to order only a slice of melon for lunch with a glass of her father's wine. Both tall and slim, they entered the restaurant. Her hair was drawn back, the bones of her face were good, her eyes were small and fixed ready for humour, for she had decided to be a spinster and do it properly; she looked forty-six and she did not look forty-six; her skin was dry; her mouth was thin, and was growing thinner with the worry about money. The father looked eighty years old, as he was. Thirty years ago people used to turn round and say, as he passed, 'That's Henry Castlemaine.'

Ben lay on his stomach on his mattress on the beach enclosure. Carmelita Hope lay on her mattress, next to him. They were eating rolls and cheese and drinking white wine which the beach attendant had brought to them from the café. Carmelita's tan was like a perfect garment, drawn skin-tight over her body. Since leaving school she had been in numerous jobs behind the scenes of film and television studios. Now she was out of a job again. She thought of marrying Ben, he was so entirely different from all the other men of her acquaintance, he was joyful and he was serious. He was also good-looking; he was half-French, brought up in England. And an interesting age, thirty-one. He was a school teacher, but Father could probably get him a job in advertising or publishing. Father could do a lot of things for them both if only he would exert himself. Perhaps if she got married he would exert himself.

'Did you see your father at all yesterday, Carmelita?'

'No; as a matter of fact he's driven up the coast. I think he's gone to stay at some villa on the Italian border.'

'I should like to see more of him,' said Ben. 'And have a talk with him. I've never really had a chance to have a talk with him.'

'He's awfully shy,' said Carmelita, 'with my friends.'

Sometimes she felt a stab of dissatisfaction when Ben talked about her father. Ben had read all his books through and through – that seemed rather obsessive to Carmelita, reading books a second time and a third, as if one's memory was defective. It seemed to her that Ben loved her only because she was Kenneth Hope's daughter, and then, again, it seemed to her that this couldn't be so, for Ben wasn't attracted by money and success. Carmelita knew lots of daughters of famous men, and they were beset by suitors who were keen on their fathers' money and success. But it was the books that Ben liked about her father.

'He never interferes with me,' she said. 'He's rather good that way.'

'I would like to have a long talk with him,' Ben said.

'What about? – He doesn't like talking about his work.'

'No, but a man like that. I would like to know his mind.'

'What about my mind?'

'You've got a lovely mind. Full of pleasant laziness. No guile.' He drew his forefinger from her knee to her ankle. She was wearing a pink bikini. She was very pretty and had hoped to become a starlet before her eighteenth birthday. Now she was very close to twenty-one and was thinking of marrying Ben instead, and was relieved that she no longer wanted to be an actress. He had lasted longer than any other boy-friend. She had often found a boy exciting at first but usually went off him quite soon. Ben was an intellectual, and intellectuals, say what you like, seemed to last longer than anyone else. There was more in them to find out about. One was always discovering new things – she supposed it was Father's blood in her that drew her towards the cultivated type, like Ben.

He was staying at a tiny hotel in a back street near the old quay. The entrance was dark, but the room itself was right at the top of the house, with a little balcony. Carmelita was staying with friends at a villa. She spent a lot of time in Ben's room, and sometimes slept there. It was turning out to be a remarkably happy summer.

'You won't see much of Father,' she said, 'if we get married. He works and sees nobody. When he doesn't write he goes away. Perhaps he'll get married again and – '

'That's all right,' he said, 'I don't want to marry your father.'

Dora Castlemaine had several diplomas for elocution which she had never put to use. She got a part-time job, after the Christmas holidays that year, in Basil Street Grammar School in London, and her job was to try to reform the more pronounced Cockney accents of the more promising boys into a near-standard English. Her father was amazed.

'Money, money, you are always talking about money. Let us run up debts. One is nobody without debts.'

'One's credit is limited, Father. Don't be an old goose.'

'Have you consulted Waite?' Waite was the publisher's young man who looked after the Castlemaine royalties, diminishing year by year.

'We've drawn more than our due for the present.'

'Well, it's a bore, you going out to teach.'

'It may be a bore for you,' she said at last, 'but it isn't for me.'

'Dora, do you really mean you want to go to this job in London?'

'Yes, I want to. I'm looking forward to it.'

He didn't believe her. But he said, 'I suppose I'm a bit of a burden on you, Dora, these days. Perhaps I ought to go off and die.'

'Like Oates at the South Pole,' Dora commented.

He looked at her and she looked at him. They were shrewd in their love for each other.

She was the only woman teacher in the school, with hardly the status of a teacher. She had her own corner of the common room and, anxious to reassure the men that she had no intention of intruding upon them, would, during free periods, spread out on the table one of the weekly journals and study it intently, only looking up to say good morning or good afternoon to the masters who came in with piles of exercise books under their arms. Dora had no exercise books to correct, she was something apart, a reformer of vowel sounds. One of the masters, and then another, made conversation with her during morning break, when she passed round the sugar for the coffee. Some were in their early thirties. The ginger-moustached science master was not long graduated from Cambridge. Nobody said to her, as intelligent young men had done as late as fifteen years ago, 'Are you any relation, Miss Castlemaine, to Henry Castlemaine the writer?'

Ben walked with Carmelita under the trees of Lincoln's Inn Fields in the spring of the year, after school, and watched the children at their games. They were a beautiful couple. Carmelita was doing secretarial work in the City. Her father was in Morocco, having first taken them out to dinner to celebrate their engagement.

Ben said, 'There's a woman at the school, teaching elocution.'

'Oh?' said Carmelita. She was jumpy, because since her father's departure for Morocco Ben had given a new turn to their relationship. He would not let her stay overnight in his flat in Bayswater, not even at the week-ends. He said it would be nice, perhaps, to practise restraint until they were married in the summer, and that would give them something to look forward to. 'And I'm interested to see,' said Ben, 'what we mean to each other without sex.'

This made her understand how greatly she had become obsessed with him. She thought perhaps he was practising a form of cruelty to intensify her obsession. In fact, he did want to see what they meant to each other without sex.

She called at his flat unexpectedly and found him reading, with piles of other books set out on the table as if waiting to be read.

She accused him: You only want to get rid of me so that you can read your books.

'The fourth form is reading Trollope,' he explained, pointing to a novel of Trollope's among the pile.

'But you aren't studying Trollope just now.'

He had been reading a life of James Joyce. He banged it down and said, 'I've been reading all my life, and you won't stop me, Carmelita.'

She sat down. 'I don't want to stop you,' she said.

'I know,' he said.

'We aren't getting on at all well without sex,' she said, and on that occasion stayed the night.

He was writing an essay on her father. She wished that her father had taken more interest in it. Father had taken them out to dinner with his party face, smiling and boyish. Carmelita had seen him otherwise – in his acute dejection, when he seemed hardly able to endure the light of day.

'What's the matter, Father?'

'There's a comedy of errors going on inside me, Carmelita.' He sat at his desk most of the day while he was in these moods, doing nothing. Then, during the night, he would perhaps start writing, and sleep all the next morning, and gradually in the following days the weight would pass.

'There's a man on the phone wants you, Father – an interview.'

'Tell him I'm in the Middle East.'

'What did you think of Ben, Father?'

'A terribly nice man, Carmelita. You've made the right choice, I think.'

'An intellectual – I do like them best, you know.'

'I'd say he was the student type. Always will be.'

'He wants to write an essay about you, Father. He's absolutely mad about your books.'

'Yes.'

165

'I mean, couldn't you help him, Father? Couldn't you talk to him about your work, you know?'

'Oh, God, Carmelita. It would be easier to write the bloody essay myself.'

'All right, all right. I was only asking.'

'I don't want any disciples, Carmelita. They give me the creeps.'

'Yes, yes, all right. I know you're an artist, Father, there's no need to show off your temperament. I only wanted you to help Ben. I only . . .'

I only, she thought as she walked in Lincoln's Inn Fields with Ben, wanted him to help me. I should have said, 'I want you to talk more to Ben, to help me.' And Father would have said, 'How do you mean?' And I would have said, 'I don't know, quite.' And he would have said, 'Well, if you don't know what you mean, how the hell do I?'

Ben was saying, 'There's a woman at the school, teaching elocution.'

'Oh?' said Carmelita jumpily.

'A Miss Castlemaine. She's been there four months, and I only found out today that she's the daughter of Henry Castlemaine.'

'But he's dead!' said Carmelita.

'Well, I thought so too. But apparently he isn't dead, he's very much alive in a house in Essex.'

'How old is Miss Castlemaine?' said Carmelita.

'Middle-aged. Middle forties. Perhaps late forties. She's a nice woman, a classic English spinster. She teaches the boys to say "How now brown cow." You could imagine her doing wood-engravings in the Cotswolds. I only found out today – '

'You might manage to get invited to meet him, with any luck,' Carmelita said.

'Yes, she said I must come and see him, perhaps for a week-end. Miss Castlemaine is going to arrange it. She was awfully friendly when she found I was a Castlemaine admirer. A lot of people must think he's dead. Of course, his work belongs to a past world, but it's wonderful. Do you know *The Pebbled Shore*? – that's an early one.'

'No, but I've read *Sin of Substance*, I think. It –'

'You mean *The Sinner and the Substance*. Oh, it has fine things in it. Castlemaine's due for a revival.'

Carmelita felt a sharp stab of anger with her father, and then a kind of despair which was not as yet entirely familiar to her, although already she wondered if this was how Father felt in his great depressions when he sat all day, staring and enduring, and all night miraculously wrote the ache out of his system in prose of harsh merriment.

Helplessly, she said, 'Castlemaine's novels aren't as good as Father's, are they?'

'Oh, there's no comparison. Castlemaine is quite different. You can't say one type is *better* than another – goodness me!' He was looking academically towards the chimney stacks of Lincoln's Inn. This was the look in which she loved him most. After all, she thought, the Castlemaines might make everything easier for both of us.

'Father, it's really absurd. A difference of sixteen years . . . People will say –'

'Don't be vulgar, Dora dear. What does it matter what people say? Mere age makes no difference when there's a true affinity, a marriage of true minds.'

'Ben and I have a lot in common.'

'I know it,' he said, and sat a little higher in his chair.

'I shall be able to give up my job, Father, and spend my time here with you again. I never really wanted that job. And you are so much better in health now . . .'

'I know.'

'And Ben will be here in the evenings and the week-ends. You get on well with Ben, don't you?'

167

'A remarkably fine man, Dora. He'll go far. He's percep-tive.'

'He's keen to revive your work.'

'I know. He should give up that job, as I told him, and devote himself entirely to literary studies. A born essayist.'

'Oh, Father, he'll have to keep his job for the meantime, anyhow. We'll need the money. It will help us all; we – '

'What's that? What's that you say?'

'I said he finds work in the grammar school stimulating, Father.'

'Do you love the man?'

'It's a little difficult to say, at my age, Father.'

'To me, you both seem children. Do you love him?'

'I feel,' she said, 'that I have known him much longer than I have. Sometimes I think I've known him all my life. I'm sure we have met before, perhaps even in a former existence. That's the decisive factor. There's something of *destiny* about my marrying Ben; do you know what I mean?'

'Yes, I think I do.'

'He was engaged, last year for a short time, to marry quite a young girl,' she said. 'The daughter of a novelist called Kenneth Hope. Have you heard of him, Father?'

'Vaguely,' he said. 'Ben,' he said, 'is a born disciple.'

She looked at him and he looked at her, shrewd in their love for each other.

The First Year of My Life

I was born on the first day of the second month of the last year of the First World War, a Friday. Testimony abounds that during the first year of my life I never smiled. I was known as the baby whom nothing and no one could make smile. Everyone who knew me then has told me so. They tried very hard, singing and bouncing me up and down, jumping around, pulling faces. Many times I was told this later by my family and their friends; but, anyway, I knew it at the time.

You will shortly be hearing of that new school of psychology, or maybe you have heard of it already, which, after long and far-adventuring research and experiment has established that all of the young of the human species are born omniscient. Babies, in their waking hours, know everything that is going on everywhere in the world; they can tune in to any conversation they choose, switch on to any scene. We have all experienced this power. It is only after the first year that it was brainwashed out of us; for it is demanded of us by our immediate environment that we grow to be of use to it in a practical way. Gradually, our know-all brain-cells are blacked out, although traces remain in some individuals in the form of E.S.P., and in the adults of some primitive tribes.

It is not a new theory. Poets and philosophers, as usual, have been there first. But scientific proof is now ready and to hand. Perhaps the final touches are being put to the new manifesto in some cell at Harvard University. Any day now it will be given to the world, and the world will be convinced.

Let me therefore get my word in first, because I feel pretty sure, now, about the authenticity of my remembrance of things past. My autobiography, as I very well perceived at the time, started in the very worst year that the world had ever seen so far. Apart from being born bedridden and toothless, unable to raise myself on the pillow or utter anything but farmyard squawks or police-siren wails, my bladder and my bowels totally out of control, I was further depressed by the curious behaviour of the two-legged mammals around me. There were those black-dressed people, females of the species to which I appeared to belong, saying they had lost their sons. I slept a great deal. Let them go and find their sons. It was like the special pin for my nappies which my mother or some other hoverer dedicated to my care was always losing. These careless women in black lost their husbands and their brothers. Then they came to visit my mother and clucked and crowed over my cradle. I was not amused.

'Babies never really smile till they're three months old,' said my mother. 'They're not *supposed* to smile till they're three months old.'

My brother, aged six, marched up and down with a toy rifle over his shoulder:

> The grand old Duke of York
> He had ten thousand men;
> He marched them up to the top of the hill
> And he marched them down again.
>
> And when they were up, they were up.
> And when they were down, they were down.
> And when they were neither down nor up
> They were neither up nor down.

'Just listen to him!'
'Look at him with his rifle!'

I was about ten days old when Russia stopped fighting. I tuned in to the Czar, a prisoner, with the rest of his family, since evidently the country had put him off his throne and there had been a revolution not long before I was born. Everyone was talking about it. I tuned in to the Czar. 'Nothing would ever induce me to sign the treaty of Brest-Litovsk,' he said to his wife. Anyway, nobody had asked him to.

At this point I was sleeping twenty hours a day to get my strength up. And from what I discerned in the other four hours of the day I knew I was going to need it. The Western Front on my frequency was sheer blood, mud, dismembered bodies, blistering crashes, hectic flashes of light in the night skies, explosions, total terror. Since it was plain I had been born into a bad moment in the history of the world, the future bothered me, unable as I was to raise my head from the pillow and as yet only twenty inches long. 'I truly wish I were a fox or a bird,' D. H. Lawrence was writing to somebody. Dreary old creeping Jesus. I fell asleep.

Red sheets of flame shot across the sky. It was 21 March, the fiftieth day of my life, and the German Spring Offensive had started before my morning feed. Infinite slaughter. I scowled at the scene, and made an effort to kick out. But the attempt was feeble. Furious, and impatient for some strength, I wailed for my feed. After which I stopped wailing but continued to scowl.

> The grand old Duke of York
> He had ten thousand men . . .

They rocked the cradle. I never heard a sillier song. Over in Berlin and Vienna the people were starving, freezing, striking, rioting and yelling in the streets. In London everyone was bustling to work and muttering that it was time the whole damn business was over.

The big people around me bared their teeth; that meant a

171

smile, it meant they were pleased or amused. They spoke of ration cards for meat and sugar and butter.

'Where will it all end?'

I went to sleep. I woke and tuned in to Bernard Shaw who was telling someone to shut up. I switched over to Joseph Conrad who, strangely enough, was saying precisely the same thing. I still didn't think it worth a smile, although it was expected of me any day now. I got on to Turkey. Women draped in black huddled and chattered in their harems; yak-yak-yak. This was boring, so I came back to home base.

In and out came and went the women in British black. My mother's brother, dressed in his uniform, came coughing. He had been poison-gassed in the trenches. *'Tout le monde à la bataille!'* declaimed Marshal Foch the old swine. He was now Commander-in-Chief of the Allied Forces. My uncle coughed from deep within his lungs, never to recover but destined to return to the Front. His brass buttons gleamed in the firelight. I weighed twelve pounds by now; I stretched and kicked for exercise, seeing that I had a lifetime before me, coping with this crowd. I took six feeds a day and kept most of them down by the time the *Vindictive* was sunk in Ostend harbour, on which day I kicked with special vigour in my bath.

In France the conscripted soldiers leapfrogged over the dead on the advance and littered the fields with limbs and hands, or drowned in the mud. The strongest men on all fronts were dead before I was born. Now the sentries used bodies for barricades and the fighting men were unhealthy from the start. I checked my toes and my fingers, knowing I was going to need them. *The Playboy of the Western World* was playing at the Court Theatre in London, but occasionally I beamed over to the House of Commons which made me drop off gently to sleep. Generally, I preferred the Western Front where one got the true state of affairs. It was essential to know the worst, blood and explosions and all, for one had to be prepared, as the boy scouts said. Virginia Woolf yawned and reached for her diary. Really, I preferred the Western Front.

In the fifth month of my life I could raise my head from my pillow and hold it up. I could grasp the objects that were held out to me. Some of these things rattled and squawked. I gnawed on them to get my teeth started. 'She hasn't smiled yet?' said the dreary old aunties. My mother, on the defensive, said I was probably one of those late smilers. On my wavelength Pablo Picasso was getting married and early in that month of July the Silver Wedding of King George V and Queen Mary was celebrated in joyous pomp at St Paul's Cathedral. They drove through the streets of London with their children. Twenty-five years of domestic happiness. A lot of fuss and ceremonial handing over of swords went on at the Guildhall where the King and Queen received a cheque for £53,000 to dispose of for charity as they thought fit. *Tout le monde à la bataille!* Income tax in England had reached six shillings in the pound. Everyone was talking about the Silver Wedding; yak-yak-yak, and ten days later the Czar and his family, now in Siberia, were invited to descend to a little room in the basement. Crack, crack, went the guns; screams and blood all over the place, and that was the end of the Romanoffs. I flexed my muscles. 'A fine healthy baby,' said the doctor; which gave me much satisfaction.

Tout le monde à la bataille! That included my gassed uncle. My health had improved to the point where I was able to crawl in my playpen. Bertrand Russell was still cheerily in prison for writing something seditious about pacifism. Tuning in as usual to the Front Lines it looked as if the Germans were winning all the battles yet losing the war. And so it was. The upper-income people were upset about the income tax at six shillings to the pound. But all women

173

over thirty got the vote. 'It seems a long time to wait,' said one of my drab old aunts, aged twenty-two. The speeches in the House of Commons always sent me to sleep which was why I missed, at the actual time, a certain oration by Mr Asquith following the armistice on 11 November. Mr Asquith was a greatly esteemed former prime minister later to be an Earl, and had been ousted by Mr Lloyd George. I clearly heard Asquith, in private, refer to Lloyd George as 'that damned Welsh goat'.

The armistice was signed and I was awake for that. I pulled myself on to my feet with the aid of the bars of my cot. My teeth were coming through very nicely in my opinion, and well worth all the trouble I was put to in bringing them forth. I weighed twenty pounds. On all the world's fighting fronts the men killed in action or dead of wounds numbered 8,538,315 and the warriors wounded and maimed were 21,219,452. With these figures in mind I sat up in my high chair and banged my spoon on the table. One of my mother's black-draped friends recited:

> I have a rendezvous with Death
> At some disputed barricade,
> When spring comes back with rustling shade
> And apple blossoms fill the air –
> I have a rendezvous with Death.

Most of the poets, they said, had been killed. The poetry made them dab their eyes with clean white handkerchiefs.

Next February on my first birthday, there was a birthday-cake with one candle. Lots of children and their elders. The war had been over two months and twenty-one days. 'Why doesn't she smile?' My brother was to blow out the candle. The elders were talking about the war and the political situation. Lloyd George and Asquith. Asquith and Lloyd George. I remembered recently having switched on to Mr Asquith at a private party where he had been drinking a lot. He was playing cards and when he came to cut the cards he tried to cut a large box of matches by mistake. On another occasion I had seen him putting his arm around a lady's shoulder in a Daimler motor car, and generally behaving towards her in a very friendly fashion. Strangely enough she said, 'If you don't stop this nonsense immediately I'll order the chauffeur to stop and I'll get out.' Mr Asquith replied, 'And pray, what reason will you give?' Well anyway it was my feeding time.

The guests arrived for my birthday. It was so sad, said one of the black widows, so sad about Wilfred Owen who was killed so late in the war, and she quoted from a poem of his:

> What passing bells for these who die as cattle?
> Only the monstrous anger of the guns.

The children were squealing and toddling around. One was sick and another wet the floor and stood with his legs apart gaping at the puddle. All was mopped up. I banged my spoon on the table of my high chair.

> But I've a rendezvous with Death
> At midnight in some flaming town;
> When spring trips north again this year,
> And I to my pledged word am true,
> I shall not fail that rendezvous.

More parents and children arrived. One stout man who was warming his behind at the fire, said, 'I always think those words of Asquith's after the armistice were so apt . . .'

They brought the cake close to my high chair for me to see, with the candle shining and flickering above the pink icing. 'A pity she never smiles.'

'She'll smile in time,' my mother said, obviously upset.

'What Asquith told the House of Commons just after the war,' said that stout gentleman with his backside to the fire,

' – so apt, what Asquith said. He said that the war has cleansed and purged the world, by God! I recall his actual words: "All things have become new. In this great cleansing and purging it has been the privilege of our country to play her part . . ."'

That did it. I broke into a decided smile and everyone noticed it, convinced that it was provoked by the fact that my brother had blown out the candle on the cake. 'She smiled!' my mother exclaimed. And everyone was clucking away about how I was smiling. For good measure I crowed like a demented raven. 'My baby's smiling!' said my mother.

'It was the candle on her cake,' they said.

The cake be damned. Since that time I have grown to smile quite naturally, like any other healthy and house-trained person, but when I really mean a smile, deeply felt from the core, then to all intents and purposes it comes in response to the words uttered in the House of Commons after the First World War by the distinguished, the immaculately dressed and the late Mr Asquith.